GRAVETIDE

RENEE JOINER

Oshun
Publications

Gravetide© Copyright 2020 by Renee Joiner

ISBN: 978-1-950378-47-0

Book design by Jes Ireland

www.jesireland.com

Published by Oshun Publications

www.oshunpublications.com

CONTENTS

Did you know you can take every story with you?

I know it's tough these days to simply find the time to relax and curl up with a good book. This is why I'm delighted to share that I have books available in audio book format.

Best of all, you can get the audio book version of any book by me for free as part of a 30-day Audible trial.

Members get free audio books every month and exclusive discounts. It's an excellent way to explore and determine if audio book learning works for you.

If you're not satisfied, you can cancel anytime within the trial period. You won't be charged, and you can even keep your audio book.

To choose a free audio book, click on your favorite title's cover to be taken to Audible's website for details.

Remember, there's no obligation to buy.

reneejoinerauthor.com/audiobooks

JOIN MY NEWSLETTER

GET UPDATES, FREEBIES & GIVEAWAYS

RENEEJOINERAUTHOR.COM/NEWSLETTER

OTHER BOOKS BY RENEE

Singles

Half Demon

Wanted Undead or Alive

Tempest

My Soul to Reap

THE RESTLESS DEAD

"Dammit!"

Jensen Mills stared in dismay at the small black line that now arched over the late Mrs. Buchanan's cheekbone. Her hand had slipped as she was applying liner to the woman's eyes, but she had doubts whether this look would get a pass in the brunch club of the afterlife. Jensen swung around, visibly irritated.

"Oh, man, sorry. I didn't think you'd scare so easily!" Her friend stood in the doorway to the room with a look equal parts sheepish and mischievous. Many things could be said of Weston O'Neill: resident bad boy, party animal, and womanizer. Most of these labels were late bloomers in his reputation, but he was undoubtedly a notorious trickster.

"I don't! You know I hate sudden jolts like that. God, I just don't understand why you do that every time I'm making someone presentable."

Weston walked over, looking down into the casket. "Presentable? She isn't really around to look at herself anymore, now, is she? I'll think she'll get a pass from the other rich housewives in the suburb."

"It's called leaving behind a legacy! Isobel Buchanan wanted to be infamous for turning a look, even in death. She might keep that reputation if I can fix this slip. Dammit, Weston! Her service is tomorrow! What will the people in attendance think?"

"That she had a sense of humor to boot. I say leave her be. This is as good as it's going to get anyway. It's all downhill from here, or rather, six feet under the hill."

"Oh, very funny..." Jensen feigned amusement. "Talking about things being as 'good as they get,' things must be working out pretty well since you've cleaned up so nicely. I thought I might be in for a double shift once you showed up."

Acting offended, Weston responded, "Are you saying I need help looking presentable?"

"Hmm. No. You're good for tonight. It came together quite nicely." Jensen smiled at him, playfully. "Are you ready for this date, or what? It's been three months! I was almost thinking of setting this up for you."

"God, I needed to scope it out myself first. This woman totally messes with my vibe. I'm not used to being charmed when I'm the charmer." He rubbed the back of his head, looking a bit hesitant. Seeing the small cracks in his confidence, Jensen knew that this girl must have been something. "Hey, um, you think she'll like me? I mean, you would date me, right?"

Jensen shrugged. "Don't know. You always had too much of a lively personality, in my opinion." She fought down a smile.

"What?! Oh really?" he mocked while failing to stop himself from blushing. "Is that why you are husband-hunting in the aisle of the departed?"

"I've always been into the quiet types, you know." Jensen

winked at him. "You better be going. That restaurant you're meeting loses open tables pretty quickly."

He checked his watch and clapped his palms together. "Phew. Moment of truth." He looked around the room. "So, um, this is your Friday? You're just keeping,"—he pointed at the casket—"her company?"

"Girls' night. She has a date with the dead, and unlike you, she can't just pull a comb through her hair and call herself ready."

"I thought you did the accounts. Listen, I know Mrs. Buchanan was excellent at spending her husband's money. Still, I don't think she is great at balancing statements."

"My office is based here, you bastard! The owner hasn't exactly figured out the digital shift yet. A lot of their stuff is still on paper. I can't take it home. Besides, the cosmetologist couldn't make it, and the old gal here needed touch-ups before her service tomorrow."

"There are guys out there who need some touch-ups too." He gave a smug little smile to emphasize his filthy mind. "You could meet someone like me."

She raised an eyebrow, looking unimpressed. "Why do you think I chose this place to start with?"

Weston laughed, merely shaking his head as he headed out. "You're hard to get, Mills. I'd love to meet the guy who can crack you."

Flipping her hair over her shoulder, Jensen taunted him. "I'm a career woman. Married to the job. Now get out before my client reports you."

Smiling, he disappeared around the corner. *Ah, Weston, she thought, always trying his luck, even if he has another lined up.*

Jensen looked back at the casket and stood with her hands at her hips. "Well, you just look fucking great, don't you? Hmm, maybe if I just—" Taking the corner of her sleeve, she rubbed gently at the black line on the corpse's cheek, working it into the foundation on the eye socket. "There we go." It was slightly discolored, but she decided it was fitting. Rumor had it that the last club meeting of the suburban housewives had ended in a few flying fists. "Sorry, Mrs. Buchanan. Blending on the recently deceased can get a little messy with a tarnished reputation."

It was safe to say that Mrs. Buchanan didn't offer much of a response.

"I just knew you'd understand."

"Oh, my God. Are you fueling neighborhood scandals?"

Looking around, Jensen nearly ruptured a vein as she saw a small, heart-shaped face peek over her shoulder. It was Maya. "Jesus, cousin. You nearly scared me to death."

Maya Foster teased a look of innocence. "What are you talking about? Look at you! You're bursting with vitality. You know, babes, when the dilemma is dead, I am known to bring a little life back to it. My timing is *just* right. Company like that will make you a bore." She looked over Jensen's shoulder to embellish her remark and took a seat on a chair opposite.

"God, I'd swear you people think I needed an intervention."

"Naturally. Darling, everything I do is totally intentional and meant to be of aid."

"Speaking of... don't you have a baby shower to plan? Your aid *there* seems vital."

Maya groaned dramatically in answer. "Don't remind me. Me and some of the girls are meeting for drinks to set some arrangements."

"Hmm. Or are you meeting for drinks because there

won't be any at the party?" Jensen placed her hand under her chin, pretending to read her cousin's intentions.

"Well, babes, like I said, *everything* I do is intentional. Which is why I thought I'd come around while I'm of a clear mind. I feel something nasty is about to happen."

"Then you should get this shower planned! Otherwise, you can be sure of bad things happening. Isn't an alcohol-free party bad enough?"

Maya rolled her eyes. "Honestly, the way you make me sound like an AA meeting waiting to happen. You are completely right, of course. I am faced with many travesties." She sighed loudly to add more dimension to her melodrama. "That is not the point I wanted to raise. Something is up with the spirits, cuz." She produced a cigarette as if out of nowhere and lit it.

"Uh, Maya, you can't smoke in here."

"Why? Is she an asthmatic?" She went on to take a puff and blew out a plume of smoke. Her response was so matter-of-fact that Jensen was left without a reply. She simply sighed and sat down opposite her.

"Well? Let's hear it."

"The souls, babes. They've been pretty restless. I know you've felt it, and don't begin to pretend that it was a malfunction of intuition. You, redheads, are too clever to fall prey to illusion. Something is up."

"Um... jeez, cuz. You really ease a woman into a conversation, don't you?"

"Come now. You work with dead people every day, and you can't handle me being direct?"

"Alright, alright. Fine. Yes, something has been off. But, Maya, I am not really equipped to be making such claims."

"Nonsense. You underestimate yourself. You're not...refined, but you have some raw skill. Besides, if you did feel it, then it means that something is definitely stirring on *the other side.*"

"So, why not go to the others with this?"

"Well, firstly, I don't tolerate pretension without class. Secondly, something about it has the shape of your energy to it." Maya's claim was so nonchalant that Jensen had difficulty taking her seriously.

She frowned before answering, "Whoa. Maya, we're speaking about hunches here. You have talents, I won't deny that, but suggesting that I have some special link to this feels almost absurd."

Her cousin took one final drag from her smoke before killing the unfinished cigarette against the bottom of her heel. She never finished a smoke. She always said it was excessive. *If you sin in moderation, then hell comes for you much later*, she always said. "Listen, cuz, all I'm saying is to keep an eye out. The dead don't have much time for us. They have places to be. So when they stop and leave breadcrumbs to premonitions and shit, I, for one, listen. You should too. I'm surprised you didn't hear that tombstone tilt over a moment ago."

Jensen's eyes went wide. "Wait, *what?*"

"Just a moment ago, in the cemetery outside. It happened while we were talking, babes. Did you really miss that? It thumped louder than my neighbor's headboard against my bedroom wall."

Jensen didn't argue. She grabbed Maya by the arm and dragged her out of the viewing room of the mortuary. Ensuring the thermostat was set to the same arctic temperature; Jensen slammed the door shut and dashed into the foyer with her cousin. She stripped off her coat, realizing the temperature difference.

"My God, cousin, that was rather rough. What's the rush?"

"Maya, don't move. I need to go have a look in the cemetery out in the back." With that, Jensen dashed to the rear exit. She was about to look for a key, but the door simply swung open at a light turn of a handle. "My God, doesn't anyone lock up before leaving anymore?"

Her cousin shouted from the foyer, "I was wondering why you were all alone. Better not let the necrophiliacs find out the place stands open at night!"

Ignoring her, Jensen rushed out through the back garden and into the graveyard. The door creaked closed behind her. All was still within the funeral home. Seconds passed by, and then minutes. The steady countdown was witnessed by the ticking grandfather clock in the hallway. The only other sounds were the rustle of leaves and the rattle of branches in the late afternoon breeze. All else was deathly quiet.

The back door burst open as Jensen rushed back in alarm. She slid behind the reception desk and picked up the receiver of the old telephone. She stood there, holding it close to her face for a moment while weighing her options. Eventually, she brought it to her ear and punched in the number of the Bayside Police Department. Someone answered, and an explanation stumbled forth between bad static and rote questioning. She placed the receiver back.

"Maya! Did you hear? Several graves have been disturbed. It must have happened only minutes ago. Jesus, I didn't know why I didn't hear anything. Some are empty. They—" There was no response. "Maya?!"

Walking back around the desk and into the foyer, Jensen saw that her cousin had disappeared.

2

DEAD MAN WALKING

Detective Thompson stood looking down into the open grave, one of several that dotted the cemetery. Jensen was irritated by the man's almost blasé investigation since being called out. He seemed uninterested and even bored for the most part. She wondered if he saw what she saw: a grave that had been dug open and trails of dark soil that slithered out of the now-empty craters as if something had been dragged from them. A large chunk from one of the tombstones had cracked off and fallen onto the turf to the side. The headstone itself was incredibly old and weather-worn. It had been crumbling for a while by the looks of it. This was evidenced by moss having grown in between the crevasses. Yet, the piece of stone would have continued resting on the corner undisturbed. It looked like it had been pushed off. Whoever had done, that must have been strong. The detective saw none of this and lazily dragged his eyes over the silent crime scene.

"Well, someone was definitely here," the detective said. "Grave robbers, looters, bored neighborhood kids without supervision."

"Neighborhood kids? I'm sorry, Detective, but the damage looks a bit extensive for a mere juvenile offense."

"I wouldn't underestimate them, Miss...?"

"Mills," she told him for the third time.

"Right, right. They're crafty these days. You said you didn't hear anything immediately? Sounds like they had plenty of time to do what they set out to."

She hadn't heard a thing, to be honest. Maya had. With her little disappearing act, Jensen couldn't bring her into this. "What happens now, Detective? How do we go about finding them?"

"Finding them?" he scoffed. "They're long gone. Nothing much to be done, I'm afraid."

"Five graves have missing bodies, and there is nothing much that can be done? Detective, whoever did this didn't just shuffle in the soil to look for some spare change. They took the bones of the buried! There must be a twisted motive."

"Listen, Miss Mills, there are a hundred twisted shits out there with motives we don't have the manpower to deal with. Look,"—he gestured around him—"no shovels, no occult markings, or any other clues—just a lot of loose ground, old rock, and open pits. No one even remembers the people that these graves belong to. The markings on the headstones have all but faded."

Jensen closed her eyes and massaged her temples. "There must be some next step we can follow, Detective."

"Didn't a grave robbery happen here a month or two ago?"

"Yes," she admitted reluctantly. It didn't happen often, but it still occurred. The caretaker had reported a couple of incidents in the last few months. "But Detective, you have to admit that this is different."

"Look, there isn't much left for me to do. Tell you what. If you see anything suspicious that could give me a solid lead, then you can let me know. Here, take this." He handed her his card. "Would you like me to escort you home? It's pretty late to be in this place all alone."

Seeing the opportunistic gleam in his beady eyes, Jensen almost cringed as she forced a polite response. "No, thank you, Detective. I appreciate the effort."

They walked back to the mortuary, and she saw the man out after two or more offers. Relieved that he was gone, she turned her attention to the crisis at hand. Before she could plot her next move, her cell phone rang. It was her aunt, Summer. "Oh, damn." Jensen wondered if she knew what had happened. She sighed, thinking her aunt probably knew everything since she was a witch.

She answered.

"Child, why did the police visit the mortuary? I felt a mortal stepping over our ley lines." Summer Hunter wasn't a woman who exchanged many pleasantries. Jensen gathered that enough time around corpses turned you into an icy bitch eventually. *Fuck, I hope she didn't sense that thought.*

"There was another grave robbery, Aunt Summer. A big one. Some of the bodies are missing. I'm not sure what happened. I couldn't convene a council until I was sure what happened. I'm only a novice."

"And did the detective shed any light on the crime?"

"No, he did not."

"How did you not hear the ruckus of the graves being disturbed?"

"There was hardly a sound from outside. If it weren't for Maya hearing the tombstone dropping outside, I would have never investigated."

"Maya Foster was there? Why did the seer pay you a visit?"

She felt her aunt was misdirected from the point. "She felt bad omens brewing on the horizon. She thought it necessary to make me aware."

The line was silent for a moment before her aunt answered. "How many graves were disturbed?"

Jensen found the question strange. "Um, five, I believe. Auntie, why—"

"I will summon the council at once. The events this evening do not seem wholly fortuitous. Expect the others to be arriving soon." With that, the line went dead.

Jensen groaned, feeling less than partial to spend the rest of her evening in the company of the Gate Guardians.

THEY WERE HUDDLED in the encroaching dark beneath the trees, right outside the gate that led to the cemetery. Summer Hunter had arrived with two senior members of the coven. They had brought along an initiate. The younger witch looked quite sullen as he stood listening to the exchange. None of them seemed particularly beneficent toward her. Off to the side, other witches stood in wait of an order. The Gate Guardians had the unfortunate distinction of being the gloomiest collective of individuals Jensen ever had the fortune of meeting. She found it hard to believe that she was one herself.

"Lenora. Desmond. It is most fortunate that the two of you decided to come." Summer didn't address them with any particular warmth, but Jensen noticed as she layered her courtesies strategically. Usually, her aunt had a rather terse way of addressing others, but she was skilled in the decorum of politics. "And I see you have brought one of our younger members along."

"The boy is here to learn. We thought he could benefit in learning from the mistakes made by others of his generation." Desmond's gray head turned in Jensen's direction, leaving nothing to the imagination as to his estimates of her.

"She looks nothing like her mother, does she?" the Gate Guardian called Lenora commented snidely. "Rather tall and the hair almost deceive you. I don't sense much of the family fire in her."

"It's what happens when we allow emotions to stand in the way of duty," the man named Desmond added disapprovingly. You risk harm from the greater cause due to selfish motivation."

Jensen didn't know if they thought her to be some meek little girl who would fold under their insensitivity or if they wanted to deliberately rouse her. Despite the harsh lash of their commentary, she stared the bastards down with a stone-faced expression. They were right. She didn't look like her mother. Instead, she had earned the stern cast and statuesque figure from her father's side. Added, she had a filthy temper to her if the circumstances were right. Regardless, she kept her composure.

Her aunt would have sensed the simmering emotion beneath her facade and decided to answer in her stead. "She has her mother's spirit and the same unfailing devotion to what she deems important." Brusque, as she was in manner, it was good to know she was on Jensen's side. "She knows her duty, which is why you stand here tonight—to fulfill yours. Earlier this evening, Mills discovered a desecration of five graves following an ominous portent. Normally, we would have discarded such an act as the work of grave robbers, but the shape of this offense is different from what we have witnessed thus far."

Desmond was the one to answer, rather abrasively. "You convened our numbers to investigate some empty pits and overturned tombstones."

The look Summer gave him in answer could have frozen hell over. "The graves are empty, Desmond, and the soil is completely upturned. I did not call you to investigate a trick by bored adolescents. I don't believe something tried to get into those graves. I believe that whatever inside was wanted to *get out.*"

Lenora stepped forward. "You make dangerous claims, Summer. What you are suggesting is—"

"I know where my views stand." Summer cut her off dismissively. "Now, I propose we fan out to search the grounds and read the magical traces left by our intruders. You have brought along a sizable number of the coven, I see. I will wait at the gate. We expect our leader as well. Hopefully, we can report our findings to him on his arrival."

Desmond mumbled something under his breath before complying. Barking orders to the retinue, four witches joined him while four others joined Lenora. Then he addressed the initiate that followed him like a shadow. "Armand, perhaps you can accompany Miss Mills on the search. Perhaps your perspectives on devotions to duty might rub off on her." Armand appeared to hold his breath for an instant before offering a stiff nod in agreement. Jensen looked pleadingly toward her aunt, but she gave a curt gesture of agreement.

The assembled parties flowed through the gate and drifted like specters across the cemetery. Armand did the same, and after a prodding look from her aunt, Jensen followed less excitedly. The dour witch nearly bolted for one of the graves at the brisk pace he was walking. It was all Jensen could do just to keep up. It was clear that he wasn't particularly fond of the idea of being paired with her. In fact, she was reasonably sure that he reserved a slight vehemence toward her. She could not be sure whether it was because of her mother's legacy or the pride-tinged bias that ran rampant within the coven. Regardless, he wasn't going to strike up a friendly banter with her.

They reached the edge of one of the disturbed graves. Focusing, Armand stretched out his hands and closed his eyes. Jensen watched him. She couldn't do it herself. Her powers had not manifested, oddly enough. She didn't mind all that much, especially looking at him. From the looks of it, a life of regimented discipline killed a personality.

Nothing happened at first, and then energy pulsed over the dirt that lay strewn around the empty crater. Tendrils of energy shot outward and snaked in the direction of the cluster of trees standing at the graveyard's edge. Jensen didn't have a good feeling about following the trail. Still, before she could share her reservations, her companion was already in pursuit. Groaning, Jensen followed. Despite her growing dislike of the man, she had to admit he had the skill for a witch in training. The other groups were still wandering close to the cemetery's center.

She finally fell into step with him. "Hey. So, um, perhaps we should tell the others of this trail. We don't really have the manpower to bolster us if we find some—"

"I can handle myself! I have been honing my practice in the last few months. I can face any challenge that besets me."

"Okay... That's great, buddy, but we're still outnumbered. Some of the others look like they've been doing this for a while. I don't think they meant for you to go off on your own if you find something."

He turned to study her coolly. "If you're so concerned, then perhaps you can report back to the others that there is a track to follow. There is little that you could offer on the excursion. I can look after myself." He stalked off.

Jensen was fuming. It was a good thing he had decided to take a walk. She was about to shove his foot in his own mouth if his actions wouldn't do it for him along the way. She watched him stalk off and wander among the tombstones. It was getting hard to see in the gloom. Jensen wondered how everyone was faring in their search without much light to go by. She turned around, deciding that she had better inform the others of the disobedient prodigy before he got himself into some real trouble.

The thought hadn't even grown cold before she heard the outcry of someone in pain. It came from behind her.

Whipping her head back across her shoulder, she saw Armand stumble, and by instinct, her legs moved in his direction. The sounds of panic continued, and then a flash of green light blazed amid the graves, casting long shadows behind the headstones that dotted them. It disappeared. She knew it was his spell. Reaching the source of magic, she saw Armand on the ground. His foot was clutched in the claw of a corpse lying on the ground. The magical blast must have forced them both down.

Jensen didn't know what to do, so she rushed to his aid. She tried to pry the skeletal fingers from his ankle, but an unholy strength made it dig deeper into his skin. The witch cried out in anguish. She saw as he raised his hands, ready to cast another incantation. Jensen wanted to shout at him to stop because they were at too close a range. It was too late. A red pulse exploded from his fingers that sent her flying backward. She was lucky not to hit her head, even though she hurt in many other places. The corpse had not flinched, but Armand was knocked delirious by his own magic.

The undead's eyes were locked on the witch, and with one strong motion, it raised itself up while dragging Armand closer. Its other hand shot out and closed around the young witch's neck. Jensen wanted to jump up and lunge at the horrific thing that had arisen from one of the graves, but it was too fast. She heard a sharp crack as the corpse snapped Armand's neck. Then it stood upright. Tatters of fabric clung to leathery skin and protruding bone, and wisps of hair dangled in the breeze. It looked at her with its hollow craters, devoid of any emotion. She expected to die then, but it turned the other way. It crawled away across the burial ground with unimaginable speed and disappeared among the trees in the distance.

Jensen sat there, breathless. She looked over at the motionless body of the shrewd young witch. It had all happened so fast. Mere seconds ago, he was filled with such fire. Now, it lay snuffed out. She couldn't bring herself to accept it. Something had to be done. She had to act. Unsteadily, she rose to her feet and started following the direction the reanimated body had sped into. Someone grabbed her arm from behind.

The unexpected grip gave her a jolt, and she turned to see one of the Gate Guardians looking at her impassively. Jensen wondered if he even noticed how tight his fingers dug into her arm. She was sure he didn't care.

Tidus Morgan stepped up from behind the watcher. She didn't know what surprised her more: the fact that he was even there, or the council of witches—spread out across among the tombstones a second ago—that suddenly clustered around her. "Foolish child. You cannot pursue that monster. You are lucky to be alive!" He was tall, broad-shouldered, and imposing; she knew him to be in his late 50s, similar to her aunt, but he looked far older. Condescension was as much a part of his long, gaunt face as the many wrinkles that lined it.

"I—I reacted," she stammered. "That thing killed him. Something needed to be done."

"And what were you hoping to do? Your powers have not yet manifested. Even a novice who *has* come into their skills knows not to attempt such danger. You *will* stay behind. You are the last guardian of the gate. Our order will not suffer the grave mistakes of your family again. Your mother was enough of a nuisance. It was merely by her unique abilities that she was even permitted to exercise her will as she did. *You* are *not* permitted the same freedoms. Do you understand?"

She met his eyes with equal intensity, restraining herself from saying things she might regret. "Can your lackey let go of my arm then?"

Tidus' eyes narrowed. Still, he looked at the man restraining her and nodded for him to let go. The man's fingers loosened, and she yanked her arm back.

"All of you go after that ghoul. It is bad enough that this boy found it before all of you. Bring it to yield. Do not let it escape deeper into the forest. *Now*." As one, the council members stepped forth into nothingness and dispersed like smoke. The coven leader followed. Only Jensen was left, together with her aunt Summer.

"God, he is such a prick."

"*Auntie*!" It was not an exclamation of shock, but more of surprise. Her aunt was always rather decorous in her display of manners. She had nearly shattered that image with her obscenity.

"My dear, I am merely stating facts. The man is an impish spirit with an insufferable ego trip ever since he was elected coven leader. It is no wonder we have been slipping in our duties."

"Seems I am the biggest failure. I feel partly responsible that this guy is dead."

"Come now. I am sure you found no cause for attachment in this overzealous pup. We have lost one among our number, but he would have hardly been a valued addition. He was far too brash. I doubt you will fall victim to much trauma." Jensen knew the truth of those words as soon as they left her aunt's mouth. She was shocked by what had happened but not scarred. "Besides, you are far more valuable. You cannot be deemed a failure if you have not been given cause to fail. There will be a time that you will prove yourself, but I doubt you will be a disappointment."

"Aunt Summer, how can you be so sure? I am past my 21st birthday. Should I not be capable of some magical feats by now?"

"Your mother didn't flower until she was 25. Then she became one of the most powerful among us." Summer offered a small smile in return.

"And she was nearly the downfall of us all." The spiteful remark came from behind. Lenora and Desmond appeared to have not been part of the search party. "She failed in her duties as a gate guardian. In allowing her worldly attachments to prescribe her actions, we lost the secrets to one of the most powerful incantations that could change the tides of this battle."

Jensen was reactive. "What should she have done? Allowed me, her own daughter, to die?"

Desmond answered, rather apathetically. "We all know our place and purpose. You should watch your tongue before addressing your superior, girl."

"What the hell is wrong with you people? Someone just died. The very witch you mentored! Are you not the least bit upset about his death?"

"The loss is unfortunate," Lenora answered dryly. "Another will take his stead. Other youths are more than capable of succeeding him." She turned to look at her companion. "Desmond, we should inform the boy's guardians. We cannot allow unwanted rumors to spread through the coven."

Desmond considered the limp body of his mentee. "Agreed." The two figures mirrored each other's strides as they approached the recently murdered Armand. Placing hands on his chest, they all disappeared into the ether.

Jensen flew around to regard her aunt. Summer Hunter had an expression that looked close to irritation. Still, her niece could see the effort she exerted in making her features unreadable. She decided to jump on the emotion before it dissipated. "Are these really the teachers I need to bring myself to respect? A bunch of blunt, emotionless, and rank-obsessed bastards that are ruthless in their devotion to magic and its laws?"

Summer sighed. "In time, you will come to understand that much of our history in witchcraft has relied on such a position toward our duty. Our unique caste, as Gate Guardians, invests us with immeasurable power and responsibility. Unlike working with the elements, nature, or the magic of expression, the boundaries on which Death operates places it on the middle ground of power. It can be as malicious as it is meant to be beneficial. The energies of

Death are potent. You have not wielded it long enough to comprehend.

What's more, as a guardian of the gate, you will be invested with power that few of us will be able to offer guidance on. The Gate Guardians' apathy is not a product of their work alone. It is a shield. It is because they are sacred. Your mother knew this. As much as I loved her, she did make choices that upset our laws. It made her volatile and unpredictable. When you are the shepherds of the deceased, that can be dangerous."

"So when will I understand? I know my power is not awakened, but I am ready. At least I can learn the secrets of the order and begin to make sense of it all."

Summer looked sympathetically at her niece. "In time, Jensen."

At that moment, a figure phased into existence. It was one member of the council's search party. Jensen found it remarkable how emotion cracked through in the face of adversity. The witch that stood before them was visibly distressed and covered in soil mixed with loose bits of leaves. She looked like she had been through hell.

Summer assumed a steely resolve. "Sister, your report. Now. What happened?"

The witch was out of breath. After recovering, she nearly fell over her words as she tried to spit them out. "Tidus and the others... They are still in pursuit of the animated corpses."

Jensen was the one to respond. "Corpses? There was only one."

"More came! It was an ambush. They...launched attacks from all sides. Our magic...it—it felt useless! It didn't harm them as we thought. We couldn't hold them back. "They...," Her words were stuck to her tongue.

"Out with it, girl! Where are the others?!"

"They took two of the council! Those monsters snatched them, and then took them away! Tidus and the others went after them. They told me to return. To give a warning. You must ward the mortuary. And the graveyard! None of these corpses must be allowed to rise, and neither must the bastion be infiltrated! I—I need to return," she stammered. "We must continue the chase!"

Summer was about to respond before the girl slipped away. "Dammit! We were more ill-equipped for this night than we imagined!"

Jensen voiced a suspicion she had formed while the girl gave her erratic report. "So the disturbed graves... They were not the work of grave robbers at all. The bones were reanimated by dark magic?"

"Yes, and it appears that Maya's premonitions, and your instincts, had some truth to what has occurred here tonight." She placed her hand on Jensen's back, gently motioning her through the iron gate that led into the cemetery. Closing it behind them, Jensen placed her hands upon the lock and muttered words under her breath. White energy spiraled from her hands across the grating and over the walls that separated the burial grounds from the morgue. The two women went back into the funeral home. Jensen found her aunt to be quite rough-handed despite the sophistication with which she carried herself. Her silver mane, usually neatly combed and in place, had assumed a disheveled look through all the excitement of the night.

Once inside, Summer closed and locked the back door behind them. "Good. That should keep a handful of unwanted visitors out. Now, we need to deal with the other handful that are not so easily rebuffed. Child, I need you to get yourself home." She removed one of her pearl earrings and handed it to her niece. "Put this on, and do not take it off until you are home. Understand?"

Jensen took the earring hesitantly, unsure of how it would help her.

Her aunt noticed her perplexity. "Don't look so dumbstruck, dear. I bestowed it with a protective charm. The smaller the object, the more potent its energies. It should keep you safe."

"Aunt Summer, what are you going to do? I can't just leave you here."

"You can, and you will. I am one of the arch magi of the council. I am fairly sure I will see this night through. I must cast an intricate spell to seal off the graveyard. Summoning the spirits is an event a novice cannot be present for. The dead are not to be tangled with in ignorance. Now go. I must get to work."

"Goddammit, stop treating me like a child. I want to—"

Jensen never finished the sentence. She was standing outside the mortuary—banished from the sanctum by her aunt's spell.

3

AN UNLIKELY ALLY

J ensen woke pretty pissed the following day. She hardly slept. It wasn't that she was plagued by nightmares or disturbing visions of any kind. She just felt pretty pathetic.

It was a feeling she wasn't particularly used to.

For years, she had been part of a coven who kept her in the dark. Granted, she was powerless when it came to magical warfare. Magic was a part of her, but it didn't yet flow through her. Her intuition was a bit stronger. Sometimes she could read magical signatures like they were a language she once understood, but that was the extent of her abilities. Yet, the Gate Guardians could observe immense potential in her dormant powers. She was a gate guardian—a watcher on the boundary between the worlds of the living and the dead. It was a legacy passed on from her mother, a heritage she did not understand. Neither did anyone seem especially keen to help her do so. Not until she could harness it. Thus, like so many other times, she was mulling over the thought while drinking coffee, trying to figure out how the hell it was supposed to be accomplished.

Her thoughts were foggy from the lack of sleep. The events from the previous night were playing through her mind. She tried piecing the moments together, filtering through the memories for any clues by which she could hope to prove her worth. They were all in a lot of crap. That was for sure. So much, in fact, that she felt it was rather insouciant for a witch to be sitting in her kitchen when her coven was facing the peril of the undead. But what could she do? She knew the problem was that she was trying to solve a witch's problems in attempting to think like one. The reality, however, was that no one had taught her how. Perhaps it was time to take a different course of action. She may not have been a full witch, but she had other skills to draw on that benefitted her well enough in her mundane life.

Finding her coat in the hallway, she rummaged through its pocket. Inside, she found the card of Detective Thompson. Walking back to the kitchen, she dialed his number on her cell phone. The attempt was frustrating. The bastard only picked up after the third call. She half-expected a reprimand. Instead, the line was quiet, save for the shallow breathing on the other end. "Good morning, Detective?"

"Miss Mills? Is something wrong?"

"Why, yes. The fact that there are new leads that are just waiting to be uncovered, and no one in the force seems over-joyed to go look for them."

"For God's sake! Mills, we found nothing suspicious on the scene last night. What damn leads could you have found in less than a day? I hope this is not some game..."

"Plenty. Tracks leading into the forest and signs of a struggle. I believe we have an escalating situation." She was playing rather coy, but she couldn't help herself. "Besides, the daylight might make you notice things that you didn't notice in the dark."

"Look, this is a waste of time. I want you to drop the case and call me only when you have some serious evidence."

"If any crime leaves some serious evidence, then it isn't a perfect crime, is it? Besides Detective, I think you know as well as I do that my dialing finger isn't shy."

Jensen heard him cursing on the other end of the line, even if he tried muffling the receiver. "Fine! I'll send my partner over to investigate these leads." That was precisely what she was hoping he'd do. "Meet him at the cemetery in 30 minutes. And...Miss Mills?"

She was smiling. "Yes, Detective?"

"Lose my damn card." With that, the line went dead.

NEARLY AN HOUR LATER, Jensen was still waiting outside the morgue's cemetery. She was leaning on the hood of her car in the street parked across the grounds' west entrance. It was the only other entrance to the graveyard, save for the south gate through the funeral home. Any additional entry could only be achieved by scaling walls or digging under them. The dead didn't seem to have trouble getting out, so she doubted it would be that hard to get in.

She itched to call Detective Thomson again, just for the sake of grinding his loins by playing the damsel in distress. Jensen was, however, not desperate to prove her point. This guy, whoever he was, was 30 minutes late. Bayside PD was not that far. Either he was seriously delayed, or he was deliberately taking his time to piss her off. She wasn't about to stick around to give him the satisfaction to know if he succeeded.

Just as she was about to climb back into her car, a police vehicle turned the corner. It parked across the street, and a young man climbed out. This is Thompson's partner? He was far younger than she expected, almost 10 years the detective's junior by the looks of it. He wasn't that bad to look at either. She would have never taken him to be a detective, though. His beach-blond hair and sun-kissed skin lent him a vitality that she could never place on the scene of a grave robbery. He also looked like the type that would rather wear much less than what he was sporting today. She reined in her thoughts just as he stepped up to her.

"Miss Mills? My name is Emerson Sharp." He was so courteous it almost hurt. Jensen couldn't fathom taking her irritation out on him. "My partner, Detective Thompson, sent me here to investigate after you called."

"Well, um, thank you for coming out, Emerson. Please call me Jensen."

"Jensen." He offered her a smile. "So, you have an interesting case on your hands. This is the place it all happened?" he said, gesturing to the cemetery.

"Yes. Forgive me for asking, Emerson, but did you decide yourself to come and investigate? I mean, what did Detective Thompson tell you?"

"Well...nothing much, to be honest. Gus was rather blunt on the phone. He basically just told me to get off my ass and see what I can do here. So, maybe you can fill in the blanks."

"It gets pretty weird. I'll have to show you."

"I can deal with 'weird.' How about you lead the way?" She still couldn't wrap her mind around how friendly and approaching he was. She started doubting whether she wanted to drop some of the freaky details on him.

A moment later, they were walking among the graves. Jensen led him all the way to the center ring, where most of the action had happened the previous night. She was about to start her story, but he was already talking after a survey of the area.

"Looks like someone was digging around without permission, huh?" He knelt closer to one of the disturbed and now empty graves. His eyes widened slightly. "Actually, it looks like something was digging to get out. The grave dirt looks like it was pushed outward, and by these marks *here*; it looks like whatever it was dragged itself to the surface. I'm surprised he overlooked that..."

Jensen raised an eyebrow. "Really? You think he should have picked that up?" She knew he should have, but she couldn't confess her animosity to this...Gus.

"Yeah. Not just that, these tracks over here. It winds right out of the grave. It's difficult to see where it leads in the grass, but something definitely moved here." He stood up then. "And this, this was pushed over." He noticed the corner piece that had fallen from the tombstone. "Shit. Whatever it was, it was strong. I'd have to put my weight behind that to nudge it enough to tip off."

Jensen was starting to see why the surfer boy had a knack for detective work. "There are more here...Your partner said it was grave robbers, but they desecrate grave sites to find something off the bodies. They don't usually—"

"Take the bodies? No, they don't. I don't think you're dealing with something normal here. Hold on." He started counting. "One, two, three... there are five. Five graves unearthed."

"Um, yes. My aunt seemed to react to that detail pretty notably as well."

He looked from one to the other, and then turned to her. "It's a guess, but judging the distance, I'd say the disturbed graves are equally spaced from one another."

Jensen frowned, not sure whether she followed. She wanted to admit it was odd, but she had not even mentioned the narrative of witchcraft. When magic got involved, everything had the tendency of being a bit weird. "Why is that significant?"

"Because they form a pattern, and anything with a pattern is normally intentional. It is why the headstones are marked as well."

"Wait, *what?*"

"Oh, yeah. Didn't you see it? Look at the corners."

Jensen did, and she recognized the unmistakable runes of witchcraft. She wasn't sure what they meant, but she felt a dormant power to them. She walked to the other tombstones of the disturbed graves. "They all have it, these markings. Why did I not notice this before? Except for this one."

"The one with the broken corner? Check the piece on the ground."

She knelt on the grass, and sure enough, a symbol was visible on the side facing up.

"I think it may be occultist."

Jensen looked back over at Emerson Allen as he stood, far too calmly, with his hands to his hips. He definitely was an off-the-beat kind of cop. "Numbers, patterns, occult markings... I get the feeling you're not new to the world of the paranormal, are you?"

He seemed to snap out of thought, almost as if he was caught in the act. "Oh, uh... Well, I've dealt with some cases."

"By cases, I am sure you don't mean breaking up a bunch of neighborhood kids toying with things they can hardly begin to understand?"

He looked rather sheepish while trying to look more

serious, but he conceded. "I've dealt with what some might call the genuine thing."

Jensen folded her arms, scrutinizing him as she walked over with slow deliberation. "So if I were to tell you all of this is real, would that rattle you? What if I told you that the things that crawled out of those holes were the dead brought back to life?"

He met her look, despite seeming self-aware. His gaze was steady, and Jensen soon realized he was reading her out as much as she was reading him. "I guess that would rattle me as much as when I'd tell you that I know you're a witch."

Jensen stopped in her tracks. She wasn't afraid, but she was on her guard. A silence followed before she answered. "How much do you already know?"

He gave a half-smile. "About this case? As much as I can see. About the bigger picture behind it? Maybe a bit more."

"So, you think you have a hunch who may have caused this?"

"A hunch? Yes. But even I am not sure. Whoever they are, they used dark magic to reanimate corpses."

"What makes you believe it is dark?"

"The tombstones of the empty graves lie in the shape of a pentagram."

Jensen was slightly taken aback. She wondered if anyone last night even noticed. A part of her was sure they did, but why would they tell her? "That wouldn't necessarily make it dark. Pentagrams have long been held as sacred symbols to the Wiccans."

"True. But anything sacred presented in its inverse becomes a profanity. It becomes an opposite manifestation of the original. When something good is taken, tainted, it becomes dark—a mockery of the original craft. Witches work in line with the natural order. Raising the dead is not natural." He looked around. "There are tracks here on the edges of the dirt that don't look like they belong to anything dead. What happened after my partner left you last night?"

Jensen was taking a chance, but she wondered where an open conversation with the detective would lead. "My aunt called, and she summoned a council of witches. We call ourselves Gate Guardians. They came and searched the grounds to find any magical traces that may have been left by intruders."

He chuckled. "So, do you folks watch these graves *after* they are dug up, or before?"

Jensen gave him a look. "None of them were here when it happened. I was the only one on the night watch, so to speak. I didn't notice anything happening until it already did."

"So what were you so busy with?" he challenged playfully.

"Being a damn rookie. I haven't really come into my powers yet. I crunch the accounts... and they let me help around with the recently deceased."

"Oh, yeah. You're the girl who does their make-up. Man...the guys at the station said their boys who had passed away in the last few months had never looked as good as they did in their caskets."

"*Anyway*, I didn't hear anything. My cousin, who came along, did. She heard something heavy fall. I guess it was the corner piece of that headstone."

Emerson considered the stone in question. "I think one of the walking dead knocked it off. The grave under it is tangled with more roots. I think it got stuck and tried to pull itself free. The stone came loose after it. Probably good too. I think it broke the spell. You might have found a whole bunch wandering about."

"Jesus! I call you here for five minutes, and you know more about witchcraft than I do!"

"If you haven't tapped into your magic yet, then why do they involve you at all?"

"Because apparently, I'm some gate guardian." She noticed him raising an eyebrow in question. "It's a legacy thing. Something I gained from my mother and sure as hell don't understand."

"Hmm." He looked contemplative for a moment. "So, one thing that bugs me is this—what happened to the bodies? Did you guys find them?"

"Yes. A watcher came back, looking as though she'd been through the trenches. They came across the undead and had a fight on their hands. Apparently, their magic didn't work against them. I only saw one of the things. It was skulking behind that grave over there. Oh...and, um, and it killed the ass I was partnered with in the search. It was strong and swift. When the watchers confronted the rest of them, two of their number were kidnapped."

Emerson nodded and looked down at his feet for a moment. She had to admit, he was very calm after just hearing a witness account of a homicide. Perhaps some people just take it in stride, she thought. It looked to Jensen like he was puzzling this out. She didn't know what to make of him. It wasn't that he failed in taking the entire situation seriously, but rather that he was accepting it all as coolly as he was that baffled her. Once he did his thinking, he looked back up. "Alright, then. It looks like we have a little mystery to solve. I think I know who we should see. What are you up to tomorrow?"

"A NECROMANCER? You're taking me to see a necromancer?"

"Well, yeah. I believe they will be a solid source of information." Emerson was laid back as he drove them through the streets of a suburb Jensen didn't recognize, one hand on his lap with the other gliding over the steering wheel. She couldn't understand why he was not on edge like she was.

"Ok, confession time. I think I've been way too accepting of you just being so knowledgeable of things I didn't even plan on telling you."

"That would be an obstruction of justice—withholding information."

"Oh, and what? If you were in my position, you would just openly confess the secrets of a coven of witches to a detective you didn't know?"

"This is Bayside, Miss Mills," he teased playfully. "Weird things happen."

"First of all, I told you, call me Jensen, please. Secondly, what we are dealing with here is not some facade of the supernatural. It's the real thing. You do realize that, don't you?"

"Why else would I be taking a Gate Guardian to see a necromancer?"

He had a good point, Jensen thought. "You do know that our covens are not on the best of terms? When it comes to the arcane arts, especially those about death, our groups have widely different views on things."

"Another reason I'm taking *you* to see one. If you, a Gate Guardian, only have one understanding of the realm of the dead, then it may be good to have the perspective of someone who deals with spirits differently."

"Ok. Enough. Out with it. How do you know so much about us?"

His thoughts seemed to drift far away for a moment before they returned. "Well, like you, I'm a legacy."

Jensen was starting to become thoroughly intrigued by this guy. "Really? In which line of witches?"

He shrugged. "Wish I knew myself. My folks passed away when I was very young. I was taken in by my aunt. She raised me, and when I was a teenager, she passed along some family heirlooms. Among them were grimoires."

"Whoa. Not even my mother left behind any of those. Usually, those books are owned by entire covens and not single families alone."

"I know. From the looks of it, my folks descend from a powerful group of witches."

"But surely, if you have contact with people in the witches' world, then someone must have given you a clue as to your lineage."

"I had the same thought, but I followed one lead after the other, and I still found nothing. The interesting thing about family grimoires is that they are enchanted to be read-only by their owners. To everyone else, they appear blank. I could see what was written, but I could hardly make sense of what I was reading. I still have them, but they're a dead end."

"Damn. You still seemed capable of figuring out quite a bit, though."

"Well, my father kept journals. Pages and pages of entries detailing much of the other sects and covens, but almost nothing of his own. I picked up a few things and made a few connections. I have enough magical sense to navigate *your* world, but not enough to understand all of it. It gets a bit rough when you're dealing with that kind of burden as a detective."

"I can only imagine." She was about to say something

else, but then they stopped in front of an old and nearly dilapidated house.

"Well, here we are."

"This? Right here? Someone lives here?"

"Nope, which is why this place is perfect. The neighborhood thinks it is haunted. That shouldn't be a problem for you, though. I can't imagine something spooking a Gate Guardian."

Jensen frowned at him, looking both suspicious and skeptical. "These necromancers are our sworn enemies. I can't bring myself to understand how one would meet us here in good faith."

"You're right, which is why we won't make your allegiances known." He gave a sly smile and stepped out of the car. Sighing, Jensen followed while feeling slightly apprehensive at his plan.

The inside was dank and shadowy. They walked into what she took to be the living room. It stood completely empty, with a dusty fireplace built into the wall opposite. Sunlight filtered through the lattices in the window facing the front yard. It wasn't much of a reprieve, but it did set her mind at ease to not be enshrouded by total darkness.

"So, where is this friend of yours?"

"She'll be here."

They waited. Five minutes passed, then 15. Even though they had not been waiting that long, Jensen felt compelled to say something. Before she could get the chance, something shifted in the fireplace. Their heads both flew in its direction. Ashes still lay strewn within. A swirling mass of it suddenly lifted until an entire cloud seemed to envelop that side of the room. It drifted for a moment before coalescing and forming a single figure that now stood in front of them. The necromancer drew back her hood, and a devious little face looked out amid loose strands of pitch-black hair. "Well, well, well, Emerson. I see you brought me more than just a curious client in search of a séance."

"Alison, this is—"

"A Mills. No need for introductions."

Jensen interjected, "How the hell do you know who I am?"

"Tsk, tsk. Seems you have no idea the history that precedes you. Don't worry, not everyone fawns over your family scandals quite as much as I do."

Emerson rubbed the back of his head. "Well, guess our cover is blown."

Alison lifted an eyebrow in reaction. "Cover? Please! Even if I didn't know anything about her, I would still have been able to tell she was a witch. Her abilities may not have bloomed as yet, but she definitely has a potency about her. I would have smelled her a mile away." She unstrapped a backpack she had been carrying and knelt down to dig through its contents. From it, she emerged with a couple of candles that she set about lighting before placing them in a circle.

Jensen and Emerson merely watched, both a bit awestruck by the witch's quick surmisal. She then cast a ring of salt around them before drawing a few quick symbols within the circle. As soon as she finished, she turned to face them. "All set. Now, Charles, I need you to step out of the ring. You can hover close by if your friend gets distressed—although no one likes a drone, so just relax."

"Distressed?" Jensen was starting to feel suspicious. "And what is this about a séance? Emerson, I thought we came here to get some answers."

"You did," answered the necromancer. "I just can't give you any myself. That would be fraternizing with the enemy.

Acting as a medium, however, is just another day of business. There are no better flies on the wall than the dead. You can ask them what you seek to know."

"As 'heartwarming' as your altruism is," Jensen responded sarcastically, "who on earth would I contact in the spirit world?"

"Why, your mother, of course," Alison responded, perplexed.

Jensen's heart sank. *Her mother.* It had been years since she had seen her or even heard her voice. The memory of her mother ended with her childhood. It was a juvenile attachment, and so much else had passed since then that she didn't even know how she felt about her. "I don't even know what I would ask."

"Well, I'm sure you'll figure it out." Alison held out her hands for Jensen to take. "Let's get started, shall we?"

"Don't you need some trinket that belonged to her to be able to make contact?" Emerson asked.

"Sure," Alison answered, "If you were just some charlatan who tried to do what we could. We commune with the dead like we do with the living, wherever they are. I'm focused enough without having to rely on costume jewelry. Which reminds me, you need to take *that* off." She was pointing at the pearl earring that Jensen still wore from her aunt. "It's a gnarly little magic block that might give you' bad reception' in the spirit realm."

Jensen hadn't even realized she was still wearing it. She took it off, looking at it for a moment before placing it to the side of the circle. "What does that mean?" Jensen asked skeptically. "Communing with them *wherever* they are?"

"Souls don't just hang around, sweetie. Eventually, they pass on. We can still reach them, even if we can't influence them when they've crossed over."

Jensen's eyes narrowed. "Really? What else can your people influence?"

The necromancer simply smiled. Like a flash, she grabbed Jensen's wrists, and the room disappeared. Jensen was bathed in light, but everything an arm's length from her was dark. *This is not your average séance*, she thought, standing there surrounded by nothingness.

Jensen... The whisper of her name echoed through that void. It startled her. She looked around, trying to figure out where it came from. *Jensen...* She couldn't place it. She wondered if the voice was being projected in her mind. She banished the thought as she turned around to see a face half-obscured by darkness. There wasn't enough to recognize it by, but she undoubtedly had the sense that it belonged to her mother.

"Mom? I..." She couldn't finish the sentence. The half-formed apparition both calmed and unnerved her. Under the enchantment of such ambiguous feelings, she couldn't get a word out.

"*Jensen...not much time... Listen to...must go... Danger.*" Her mother's words faded in and out of existence. It was like a door was being opened and then closed to a room in which a musician was playing. "*Close the gate...find the key...*" The incomplete statements drifted disembodied through the air.

"I don't understand! Mom, what gate? What key are you talking about?"

"*You must listen for... You will know...cries of the souls.*"

A deep thrumming began to overpower her mother's voice. Jensen was sure that the connection was being disrupted by an outside force. It was soon as though the air was being drawn out from that empty pocket and pulling her along. The distance that separated her from her mother grew, and the last thing she saw was her mother's outstretched hand before she disappeared.

The sensation of returning to the realm of the living was like one's consciousness falling back into a waiting body. The weight of her soul made her knees buckle, and she found herself on the floor.

The necromancer stepped out of the circle, her eyes wide. Whatever arrogant demeanor she had arrived with had all but disappeared. Around her, it appeared like the granules of salt had been shifted. The outline was wavy and nearly broken in some places. Something had tried to break the salt barrier, Jensen knew. It must have been a powerful spirit. She shuddered to think what would have happened when it broke through.

"So, it's true!" Alison gasped. "It exists..."

Emerson rushed forward and knelt beside Jensen. She looked up, confused, and was about to ask the medium what she meant, but the same ash by which the necromancer had come enveloped her. Before a question could cross Jensen's lips, Alison disappeared, leaving her and Emerson alone within the abandoned building—at least to their knowledge.

From the doorway, sinister eyes leered at the two of them right before it disappeared into the shadows.

4

THE REAPER'S KEY

The minute they stepped outside, Emerson threw open the trunk of his car. From it, he took out an old gym bag. Jensen still felt drowsy after being yanked back from the spirit realm so suddenly. She walked over to him as he dug in the pouch and drew forth an old journal.

"That's an odd place to put a book, don't you think?" she asked.

He had way more energy than she was ready for at that moment. "Nope! It's the last place anyone would go digging around for this." He held up the book, and as he closed the trunk, he placed it on top and flipped through a couple of pages before resting his finger on one.

"There! That's what you were describing, I think." His finger was pointed at a sketch of a small building with gothic architecture. Studying the drawing, Jensen was sure that what she was looking at was a mausoleum. The same one she had seen just moments before the vision of her mother was ripped away. As she was pulled back through the veil, she realized that the surrounding darkness was the inside of a tomb they had both been standing in. as she drifted away, the stone arches of the entrances rose around her before the entire building moved further and further away into oblivion as she returned to the land of the living.

"I think you're right."

"And your mother mentioned a key, didn't she?!" Emerson exclaimed excitedly.

"Yes, she did."

He slammed the book shut. "I know where to go. We can talk on the way, but we need to hurry!" He ran around the car and jumped into the driver's seat. Confused, Jensen was far more sluggish as she got in on the passenger side. Emerson started the car, and they sped off. "I need you to tell me all you know about the Gate Guardians."

"Emerson, I honestly don't know a great deal. I'm not completely a witch yet, remember?"

"I know, I know. I'm not talking about anything related to magic. What I meant was your history."

Jensen envied Emerson's handling of the situation. He seemed able to effortlessly make connections and formulate synopses regarding everything. Simultaneously, she felt bombarded by loose bits of information and memories of events that did not add up in her mind. He was a detective, though, so she might as well use her human resources at this point. "Well, as you know, witchcraft is divided into different branches of magic: druidism, elemental magic, divination, and light magic, to name a few. They are different paths that our kind follows either by choice or by birth."

"Mm-hmm. Yeah. Got it…"

She was rattling through her mind and the old teachings from her aunt. It reminded her of the earring in her hand, taken off during the séance. She placed it back in her ear, for what it was worth. "Every kind of magic has a unique function. Some use it in protection, some use it in offense, some use it to gain foresight and knowledge, and others use it to keep a balance. Gate Guardians fulfill all those roles; however, none are as significant as the duty of keeping or restoring the balance between the living and the dead. So, our affiliation with all other witchcraft is neutral. We are not nearly as concerned by the dealings of other covens as they are concerned with us. Our primary purpose is keeping watch over the dead and ensuring that the living does not interfere with them—by bringing them back or harnessing the energies they leave behind. The watch is perpetual, so when wars erupt between mortals or between witches, we take the middle ground. Therefore, we may appear...standoffish, even emotionless."

"You're not that way, though. You seem to have a lot of fire and spunk."

"Well"—Jensen blushed and cleared her throat—"as I said, I'm not a full witch. My aunt said I would understand the burdens of our duties *one day*. Our vigil is over the realm of the spirits, which is a silent watch more than anything else. The departed may leave us hints or impressions of what happens in the spirit world, but we cannot speak to them directly. We could once, but the art is forbidden."

"But the necromancers can?"

"They are not allowed to, which is why we are at odds with them. Spirits are driven by emotion, not logic. Many of their intentions may be selfish because they feel stuck when they have not passed. If we allow ourselves to listen to their whims, we become subject to them. How we react may then upset the balance. Our purpose is to ensure that they remain in the spirit world. Their energies are powerful when not bound by mortal flesh. Therefore, they cannot reenter our world. It cannot be allowed. Our protective role comes in by ensuring that other witches do not tap into their realm to harness their power. It is only then that we may go on the offensive."

"But why watch over burial grounds then? If souls have left their mortal vessels, then why do you guys usually entrench yourself near graveyards or funeral homes?"

"Because the bones of witches retain a connection to their souls. Therefore, they are imbued with the potent magical energies that can be recycled and used for powerful spells by living witches with ill intent. Mortal flesh contains power and brings it under control. Without it, that energy is almost volatile and needs to remain buried—until the soul has passed on. They are almost like batteries that need to reach their expiry date."

"Well, damn. You knew more than you let on."

"That's just history. I'm still having a hard time connecting the dots as to the things happening now. Obviously, someone is messing with the dead, but we still don't know who. After my mother's warnings during the séance, I now believe that the looming threat has something to do with her legacy."

"It may have everything to do with that."

His comment surprised her. "What do you mean?"

"I think you were a bit spaced out, so you may have missed Alison's strong reaction after you lost connection with your mom. She said, 'it exists,' and I think she was talking about the key. It also makes me think that she was tuning in on your meeting in the nether realm. Come to think of it, I think it's the only reason she agreed to meet us."

"To spy. Did you know she was going to do a séance?"

"No, although I wasn't sure. They can talk to the dead, so she may have asked them what they knew. I thought she'd at least be able to help us with some information. If the dead were raised, then a necromancer might know how to read some of the clues. Some are capable of doing it."

"That is why they are a nemesis of the Gate Guardians. They are a taint to the path by doing the things that are forbidden."

"You didn't mention necromancers once, though. Neither did your coven in their suspicions."

"No. I think we all discounted the idea when we saw the monstrosities they raised. So, with Alison knowing about the key, what do you think she'll do with that information?"

Emerson tensed his jaw as if trying to consider the possibilities. He then answered, "I don't know, but I don't have a good feeling about it. This is why we need to find it first."

A memorial graveyard met them as they turned the corner. Marble tombstones were plotted out symmetrically over a green lawn that seemed to stretch out into eternity until it touched the horizon. It dotted the hill's upward incline and plateaued into a city of crypts, tombs, and sepulchers. Somewhere among that slate and granite jungle lay the mausoleum they needed to find.

They parked and walked up to the entrance. A man was seated in the guardhouse and gave them a passive look of an acknowledgment as they entered. Still, Jensen noticed as he spared her a lingering glance just long enough that she became mistrustful. Looking at him, he seemed familiar. Something about his demeanor was faintly reminiscent of the evening they investigated the supposed grave robberies. As they ventured in between the rows of ivory headstones, she felt almost sure he had been there the night of the council. It wouldn't have surprised her. Gate Guardians were stationed in all such places.

As they climbed over the hill, they were surrounded by

the older parts of the graveyard. Monuments arose around them as tributes to the chivalry of heroes or the megalomania of family pride. It was an impressive sight. She wondered if others sensed the energies of spirits pouring forth from the stone. It felt very alive, despite being home to the dead. She shuddered to think what would happen if they opened themselves to the choir of whispers. "Do we even know where we are going?"

"I do. I've been here before," said Emerson matter-of-factly.

Of course, he has, Jensen thought. "To stare at the edifice, your father had drawn in his journal?"

"Oh, I've tried to get in, but a lock seals the door that I could never open. Not even by force."

"And this key is inside? Seems ironic. How are *we* supposed to get in then?"

"Being a gate guardian, I was hoping that would be where you came in. And...There it is. We should—" The look of excitement turned into despair before he rushed to cover the distance that separated them from the tomb. Jensen sprinted after him. As they reached the front face of the mausoleum, she understood his shock. The heavy wooden door that had deterred him from entering the last time now lay unhinged on the lawn.

"Shit!" He rushed forward and through the entrance. Jensen followed and nearly stumbled over the blasted rubble and loose stone that lay strewn over the tomb's floor. Small craters became visible with the sunlight filtering through, as plaques had been destroyed to reveal the bones buried within the wall. Someone had been here, and their search had been frantic and desperate. Whatever their intentions and she was sure there was only one, they made no effort to conceal their defilement of this burial place.

"God. Guess someone had the same idea as us."

"Yeah, but they had no idea where they should be looking," he responded, notably more calm than he had been before he charged in.

"You sure? They seemed to be pretty convinced that it was behind one of these wall graves."

"As they would. This is a monument for your people."

"The Gate Guardians?"

"The gate guardians."

"You have to be kidding me."

He looked at Jensen, a bit surprised and even slightly bemused. "They really didn't tell you much about your heritage, did they?"

She shrugged. "Guess it's lucky that we met then, isn't it?"

He smiled and opened his arms wide in gesture. "Well, if my father's journal is anything to go by...welcome to the resting place of your ancestors."

Jensen looked around. The place had been completely trashed. Yet, amid the rubble, dust, and dislodged bones, the ornate carvings on the cornices and the pillars that framed the wall graves were fairly beautiful. With that knowledge, she expected to have a feeling of awe, at the least, in being surrounded by her history. Sadly, so little had she been told thereof that she could not bring herself to feel attached to the faint magical traces that surrounded her.

"I'm surprised that none of the bones are missing. They've just been flung around."

"Well, I may be a novice, but I can sense enough magic to know when a place has mystical significance. There is no magic left here, though. If these were the gate guardians, they, above all, should know how to pass on after death. Their souls would no longer have any ties to the living. If these bodies were to be raised, they would merely be sluggish, empty vessels. The dark energy used to animate them would be wasted. Saying that, are you certain the key would be here?"

The teasing glint in his eye and the slight smirk across his face was enough of an answer. "If you were to hide something—and by that, I mean, hide it well—then you wouldn't make a show of how you go about protecting the place it is hidden in."

"I don't follow."

"If this tomb was packed with latent energies from witches who haven't passed on, then it would act as a beacon. Similarly, if this place was shrouded by a hundred protective spells, someone might wonder what is kept inside. The more security there is around something, the more value is announced by what is being kept safe."

"Alright. But tell me this, Detective, why would there have been a protection spell on the door to keep it shut?"

"Because it acts as a double deception. It invites them in by convincing them there must be something of value in here..."

Jensen caught on. "Until...they find out that there isn't, making them believe it is somewhere else."

"Exactly! They cracked these wall graves open, thinking that the key must have been buried with one of the guardians who used it."

"But it was never with any of them, so they realized this was a trick."

"Was it, though?"

She wasn't ready for his rebuttal. Perplexed, she frowned at him. "You are seriously confusing me right now. Obviously, their search was in vain. Besides, I don't see why the keepers would seal a key behind a marble slab if they might need it when times are desperate."

"They wouldn't. They would hide it in the most unassuming place, one which is far easier to access." He looked down one of the passageways that opened in a lit chamber with a sarcophagus at its center. Unlike the spoiled graves that surrounded them, its slab had merely been slid aside to reveal the bones of its occupant.

"That is the resting place of the first gate guardian." Jensen read the inscription on the dais and her eyes widened. "The first one in my family line. But... no. They found nothing here. Otherwise, they would not have disturbed the bones buried in the walls so violently."

"This is why it makes sense. To hide something, you place it in the most unassuming place imaginable. Sometimes, that is right in front of someone. My father wrote, in his journal, that 'the key lies in the hand of a guardian.'"

They were standing over the sarcophagus, looking down on the remains. "Emerson, it isn't here. There is nothing buried with these bones."

"He wrote in his journal that your people were very literal in their approach—in everything that they did. I don't think that they were very fond of riddles. Still, they mastered the art of creating them. Death is pretty straightforward. I think when they say a key is in the hand of a guardian..." After studying the knucklebones, he bent down, raised the skeletal hand, and singled out the index finger—where the bone ended in the ridged and serrated shape of a key.

Jensen gasped.

FOR THE FIRST TIME, Jensen felt like she was at the center of a supernatural conflict. Despite her apparent lack of power, most of the unfurling plot revolved around her bloodline history and her coven. Not that she could count on the support of many of them. Instead, she had the help of an offbeat detective who hid his knowledge of the paranormal behind the guise of normality.

Whether by destiny or merely dumb luck, Emerson Allen was a mediating force connecting the mystery's disparate parts that surrounded the Gate Guardians' misadventures. No sooner had they found out about an artifact that they didn't even think of before today, than he was already onto the next clue. In the mausoleum, he had noticed that the first keeper in her family line was a monk. Once again, he had miraculously made another deduction based on his father's archival of other witches' secrets, and they were off chasing the next big lead. Jensen just didn't understand what was happening with Emerson's other investigations while he was playing around in a world where he wouldn't be able to file a scrap of evidence. She was sure he wasn't on the payroll to uncover the wiles of witches—which was an injustice, considering how good he was at it.

After finding the key, something had come over him to search the rest of the mausoleum. Even though the guardians' resting place had been defiled, it nevertheless unearthed treasures that aided two people who didn't have any help in navigating the world of witchcraft. The bodies had been buried with scrolls preserved in sealed marble cylinders. The ancient texts were written in an unfamiliar script that neither could translate. However, he still managed to recognize through his father's notes. He was sure they were individual accounts of each guardian's watch —secrets they carried to their grave. Jensen had made a mental note to have a look through his father's journal herself if he'd allow it. It had brought him into contact with the most unlikely people located in the strangest of places, such as the one at which they had just arrived.

"Emerson, I have to tell you if your father's notes brought us here, then the mystical world is more unorthodox than I ever imagined." She was skeptical as they stood facing a grotto. A cave had been carved into the cliff face, and a holy shrine was set inside. Reliquaries dotted the shelves niched into the rock. Simultaneously, lamplight was set to the back of the heads of statues depicting angels and saints. Every stony face was donned with that golden halo, and their lifeless eyes looked down on the dais and the platforms upon which the religious left their hopes and sorrows. It was a place of gathering and prayer. Close by was located a monastery and a chapel.

"The Wiccan world is gravely misunderstood, my child, even by those who have studied it for years." The voice didn't belong to Emerson but instead came from their left. Both of them turned as a man walked up the stairs, the hem of his burgundy robe flowing over the stone steps behind him. It made his movements almost spectral. Jensen could hardly discern whether his legs moved underneath the fabric as he drifted toward them. She barely heard his footfalls on the stone.

"Brother Ambrose," Emerson addressed him politely, "thank you for meeting with us at such short notice."

Never in her life would Jensen have thought such a laid-back looking guy to be so well-mannered. There was an odd sophistication to the detective that belied the attitude that she had come to expect from him by the manner of her first impressions alone. She began to think that it was all part of a great disguise.

The elderly friar gave a gentle smile before he answered. "Always tied to such decorum. "You know," he said to Jensen, "the first time this young man came to my door, I was almost certain that a haughty arrogance would be inextricably tied to his character. It is amazing the perceptions cultivated when dealing with young witches. Yet, he is possibly one of the most humble men I have ever met for all his wit and skill. That is saying something significant, considering I live in a monastery with 50 of them."

"God, you live in the monastery with 50 other young male witches?" It slipped out of her mouth before she could stop herself, and her face flushed scarlet. She sometimes wished she could control the involuntary actions of her tongue. Being coy with a monk could not bode well when one sought his aid, and she had used the name of the Lord in vain.

The rising tension inside her shattered almost immediately as both men started to laugh. She felt her cheeks burn in the heat of her shame. To her surprise, the friar was even ready with an answer. Grinning, he replied, "The doors to the home of our Lord are open to anyone, my dear. In my experience, young witches seek out beds that are very different from the ones we can offer." He winked at her playfully before resuming the propriety befitting his role. "Now, as much as an old man would like to prattle about a hundred mediocre things, I do sense your quest is one of urgency."

"Yes." The humor melted steadily from Emerson's features as he drew forth the key and the bag of scrolls he had collected from the tomb of the gate guardians. "Brother Ambrose, we have a lot of questions. I don't know where to begin."

The friar's eyes sparked with such life that the age had

almost dissipated from his features. "Well, child, allow me to start, then. If what you are holding in your hand is what I believe it to be, then your life is in great peril." He stared at the trinket in Emerson's hand until his features contorted in pain, and he pressed his hands to his head.

Neither of them understood what the cause was, but by intuition alone, Jensen instructed, "Emerson, put it away!" She stepped forward to help.

He did. As soon as the key disappeared, Brother Ambrose opened his eyes and considered them anew. His tone was urgent. "Keep it concealed! If the wrong eyes should see you have this…" He was still recovering. She suspected that some dormant power in the key had awakened that did not agree with him.

"Forgive me, Friar Ambrose," Jensen said, "but I cannot see how. Few would even know what this was if they saw it."

"My dear, that is unmistakably the Reaper's Key. One simply needs to have heard of it and felt its power to be able to recognize it. Do you not sense the energy that flows from it?"

Jensen and Emerson looked at each other and then back at the friar, baffled. The friar looked unnerved. Motioning for them to follow him, he led them to the inside of the shrine. The central reliquary held a marble statue of the Virgin Mary. Ornate gold frames encased crystal glass panels, and the entire container rested upon a sandstone tiled platform.

They walked up the display, and the two young people watched as Brother Ambrose bent before the Virgin Mother and placed his hand upon one of the tiles on the edge. There was the momentary sound of stone shifting underneath, and the reliquary started moving to the side. An opening revealed itself beneath the relic, and stairs descended into darkness.

The friar stood up and then walked into the secret entrance. As his head disappeared beneath the opening, Emerson and Jensen didn't need instruction to know they should follow. As they entered, the stone shifted back into place above them, and all was enveloped in darkness. Unexpectedly, a suffused glow filled the passageway they stood in as light emanated from the niches set in the wall. The detective leaned against it to have a closer look and faced Jensen with a gleam of astonishment in his eyes. "Crystals. They're crystals, but how...?"

"This place draws from the magic of those who enter. It will only ever set alight for the likes of the mystically inclined." The friar took the lead, and they were guided down the passageway until it opened into a large cavern. They were standing in a catacomb. The subterranean burial place was flooded with the same pale light as the hallway. From it branched other passages—galleries lined with recesses containing sacred remains. For a girl who had seen her fair share of graveyards, Jensen was impressed. She could feel her untrained senses tingling in the presence of so many of the dead. She wasn't sure why she felt it more strongly here than anywhere else, but she was sure it was because many of the souls had not passed on.

"Now we can talk without fear of being discovered." He turned to regard Jensen. "I suspect, my dear, that you must be a Gate Guardian—not a watcher of just any kind either. If you have the Reaper's Key, then you must be a gate guardian. I am surprised that you are unable to sense the intense signature of the artifact." He looked at Emerson then. "Mr. Allen, would you mind handing the key to our friend? I have a suspicion that she has never held it herself.

Perhaps that would explain your muted response to the issue at hand."

Emerson was stunned. "You're right. She hasn't." Digging in his pocket, he drew forth the key wrapped in his handkerchief. He handed it to Jensen. "I was so busy figuring out the clues, I didn't even consider allowing you to test whether you could make something of it."

The wrapped artifact lay in her hand. "It's alright. I didn't think of it myself, probably because I didn't see the use."

"Open it, child." The friar gestured. "The incantations within this place should contain its power for a time. The raw energy will not bombard anyone's senses here. Hold it in your hand and tap into its latent energy. Make a connection."

She carefully unfolded the material as if treating a fragile object. The rough edges of the skeletal key were accentuated in that dim light. Small runic symbols were carved into its side. Apart from that, the key had been shaped roughly from the finger bones of the witch it belonged to. It was relatively small and unobtrusive but did not fail to emit the impression that it was a token of incredible power. A power that she only now began to sense. Her other hand reached out almost organically with her fingers drifting over the key momentarily before grazing its edges. Her breath caught as her consciousness was spirited away.

A vision flashed before her eyes. A large wrought-iron gate loomed before her, surrounded by fog and midnight. Its locks were sealed. Within that darkness, wandered specks of light. Each drifted toward the mists that parted at their entry, with wispy tendrils wrapping around the ethereal shapes that encased them. Human forms became visible. They were souls. More and more moved to the gate until the mist started to glow. The emission became blinding and burned her eyes as she tried to avert her gaze. But she was forced to look on—forced to witness the closed gates that prevented the piled masses of the dead from passing on.

The vision disappeared, and Jensen gasped for breath.

"God, are you alright?" Emerson asked, sounding alarmed.

"The gate...through which the souls pass. I saw it. It is shut! And this..."

"Is the key," the friar offered, completing her thought. "Your vision is troubling. The fact that the key lies in the hand of two novices makes the situation all the dangerous."

Emerson felt alert. "Brother Ambrose, you keep talking of this danger, yet we have no clue what we should be looking out for."

"Your father's journals...Did they ever mention anything about a Gravetide spell?"

"No, it didn't. But—"

"But the Gate Guardians did," Jensen interrupted. "I overheard them in one of the councils. They always became very grim at the mention of it, as if it was some lingering threat. It came up every time they spoke of my mother."

"It was because your family line was the only witches that could ever hope to prevent it from being cast. As Gate Guardians, your purpose is to ensure the passage of souls into the next world, regardless of what that may mean for the departed witch in question. Before they pass through the gate, they wait, and they wander, lingering due to a tie in the realm of the living. When witches stay behind, their magic remains connected to this world. It runs the risk of being harvested by those with malicious intent."

"We know. It is why the Gate Guardians exist. Our coven

prevents the dead from rising or banishes back their spirits if they find a loophole to return."

"Yes, but one soul does not compare to a hundred," the friar explained. "What else did you see in the vision?"

"Spirits. Souls desperate to move on but herded in front of the shut gate. They have become restless. They want to be free, but they cannot pass into the next life."

"Then it is as I feared." The friar shook his head and closed his eyes. "The dead have been blockaded. I believe it was part of some witch's plan."

"Through this...spell? The Gravetide spell?" Emerson asked.

"The spell allows the caster to tap into the magic of not just one, but all souls who have not crossed over. Herded as they are, their mingled energies localize to a single point, which can be accessed by the purposeful direction of one's magic. To accomplish this would take immense power, and they would need a conduit by which to channel those energies."

"The key..." Jensen affirmed in a hushed tone.

"I suspect so. The Reaper's Key was meant to unlock the dead's gates and ensure that souls pass on freely to the next life. A dark practitioner would seek to overturn that purpose by using it in casting a spell that would seal them off from the next realm forever. Once accomplished, the power that would have fueled the gates' opening now lies unused within the key. With it, the wielder can cast the blood spell instead. It harnesses the sanguine energies within the caster, making it vibrate to a frequency similar to those that fill the restless soul who cannot cross over. It ties the witch to the essence of the lingering spirits, and then this essence can be fed on. The spirit starts to wither and decay, and this allows the caster of the Gravetide spell to siphon the residual magic that the dead witch left behind."

"Fuck!" she said. The jaws of both men nearly dropped to the ground. She didn't care. The friar was a witch, after all. She was sure he cursed more often than he let on. She met their stare but continued unperturbed. "They knew! All of them knew. Yet, they still downplayed it until it was too late."

Emerson was the one to respond. "You're talking of the Gate Guardians, aren't you?"

"Yes. Dammit, Emerson. They've deluded themselves into thinking they can do this alone, but they need to involve other covens. This could overthrow the delicate balance of witchcraft as we know it."

"Brother, is she right? What are the repercussions of this spell on the supernatural world? How would the balance be upset, exactly?" the detective asked.

The friar placed his hand to his chin and contemplated the best way to answer. "For every witch that dies and then passes on, the energy given by the cosmos flows back into nature from whence it came. When a new witch is born, this power is bestowed unto them. In this way, nature elects its practitioners of the mystical arts by the edicts of universal law. This spell, this abomination of the law, seeks to upset that cycle. By destroying the spirits of witches who are unable to cross over, the lingering energy is stolen."

Understanding, Jensen interceded. "So no new witches are born. The energies meant for the progeny of witches are taken. And without a new generation of witches to continue the legacy—"

"Witchcraft may become extinct," Emerson concluded. A foreboding filled the space between them as the ramifications of the suspected crimes were becoming apparent.

The friar nodded solemnly. "Whoever lurks in the shadows, and seeks to undo the fabric of the natural order, must be stopped. Somehow, you must make the Gate Guardians understand, Miss Mills. By whatever means, they must display a relentless devotion to protecting you. Your role in the saga is no longer a passive one. By finding the key and wielding it as a gate guardian, it is inextricably tied to you. Whoever comes for it will now also come for you."

A chill ran down her spine, and she swallowed hard. She looked at the key in her hand, which now almost seemed to thrum with a vindictive fury at the energy that was within. To her, it also seemed as though the runes were glowing. On second glance, another rune had also appeared among the others. A mark that seemed to be temporary but no less significant. The curve of its strokes unsettled her, and she held it out to the friar.

"Brother, this mark... What does it mean?"

The elderly monk scrunched his brow and intensely studied the new symbol. The look he gave did little to soothe her, and her heart nearly sank as he said, "It means...sacrifice."

5

HELL HATH NO FURY

The silence in the car was deafening. They both knew that they had discovered a lot more than they had bargained on. Brother Ambrose seemed to know plenty about the coven holding vigil over the dead, as well as the many threats that they faced. Emerson had left him with the ancient scrolls; he promised to have an answer as soon as his research permitted it. Time was of the essence. The reasons why the Gate Guardians had been on edge was likely due to the upcoming blood moon, he had said. It was aptly named, as blood spells were said to be enhanced by the celestial energies. The lunar event was set to happen within the next three days, which means they had lost three while investigating the mystery. She doubted that the coven had unearthed nearly as much within the elapsed time, and it unnerved her, especially in light of the lack of trust that they placed in her.

As Emerson was driving them back into town, Jensen had tried to re-establish contact with her coven. She was trying to call her aunt, but there was no answer. Jensen groaned in frustration after the seventh try and then gave up. She leaned back in the passenger seat, visibly frustrated and near exhausted. The exposure to magic and spurts of clairvoyance was taxing on the untrained witch. Emerson noticed, and perhaps after looking for the right words, he broke the silence.

"Hey, I know this is a lot to take in. We are in a bit of a tight space, knowing what we know while being the rookies. You have to hand it to us, though. For two people who have yet to come into their powers, we have done a hell of a lot more than the douches that are senior within your coven. I am sure we'll get through this if we keep on using those street smarts."

"I just—I don't understand how a mystical relic so potent could tie itself to a novice witch. I mean, you held it in your own hand far longer than I did, and it still bonded to me. It would have been a hell of a lot safer in your keeping. You seem to know your way around all this crap. Perhaps if I just didn't feel so powerless, I would know what to do next. I don't even know if I'm afraid, to be honest. I'm just anxious to get things done!"

"Man, this really did a number on you. Look, I don't want to intrude, but I could...stay over? Sleep on the couch. Just to make sure you'll be ok until we can reach your coven."

Emerson's offer was sweet. She found it amazing that he could be so calm and even considerate in the face of adversity. She would have been blazing by now. It was just her temperament. She sometimes thought it was a blessing that her abilities hadn't manifested. Recklessness was a default for her when things got too heated.

She tried to relax a bit before she answered. "Thanks, Emerson, but I'll be fine. Look, I have your number. I'll call if something is up. If I do get hold of the coven, I suspect it'll be better to keep you out of any ensuing confrontation. They'll be on edge finding out what we know, and they wouldn't take kindly to a legacy witch knowing of all this if he's not a Gate Guardian."

"Damn. So you won't be telling them about me? Very rebellious," he teased.

"Well, I guess it was high time that *I* was allowed a few secrets." She winked at him, and he smiled, blushing slightly. Law enforcement could take a few notes from him, she thought. He was alright.

They stopped in front of her apartment building. Jensen climbed out and turned to thank him. "Hey. The same goes for you. Give me a shout if things go south on your end. I'll... update you tomorrow?"

He flashed a bright smile. "It's a date! You keep safe now, Miss Mills."

She playfully narrowed her eyes at him before he drove off. Afterward, she headed up to her apartment. Climbing the stairs was a hassle. She could hardly believe how much the last few days had tired her out. Walking into her place, she was almost thankful for the momentary reprieve the sense of home offered her.

However, the feeling wasn't long-lasting. Settling in, she could immediately sense that something was wrong. The hair on the back of her neck stood on end as the warped energies of the room reached her. She had never felt anything like it before. She stepped forward cautiously, uncertain of what awaited her. Nothing happened. Minutes passed. Eventually, the feeling subsided enough for her to discount it as mere nerves.

She took a shower and washed off the day and all its impossible expectations. In those simple rituals, she began to feel more human and less burdened by the challenges

that were set to her. Climbing into bed felt almost instinc-
tual, but she did not plan on falling asleep when she did.
The sweet release of slumber merely came for her and took
her mind to places where the imbalances of power didn't
threaten to overtake her.

It all changed in a heartbeat. Her eyelids flew open and
were met by total darkness. As her intention shifted toward
switching on her night-light, her muscles were unresponsive. She lay there, unable to move, her eyes directed to the
void of her ceiling. Suddenly, her chest became heavy, and
the weight of something alien straddled her. A face slid into
view, obscured by the gloom with only the dark shape of a
deformed head to give her an inkling as to the nature of her
offender. Realizing what loomed over her, her mouth
shaped the sound of a scream that never left her lips. It was
a demon.

Spiny fingers violated her as it crept up her sides. Its
touch was like the rough kiss of sandpaper and that of ice
being placed against her skin. The slither of its hands was
unbearable as it finally reached her neck, and she felt the
sting of claws piercing her flesh. Needle pricks became
stabs, and a piercing cold became a lancing fire. She closed
her eyes, and by sheer force of will forced herself from that
moment. She bolted upright, gasping, and clutching at her
throat. The room's light was still on, but the sense of dread
had not left the room. She could not go back to bed.

Jensen did not waste time to grab for her phone and try
to call her aunt. "Oh God, Summer Hunter, pick up!" There
was no answer. "Where the hell are you?" she screamed at
her phone.

Several attempts yielded the same result until she
resigned herself to the desperate bid to call on her coven
leader. It would be against the direct wishes of her aunt, but

she could no longer protect her. Too many forces were at play. She dug frantically through the drawer in her dresser and pulled forth a black candle. She was not supposed to own one. It was an item reserved for full witches to call upon aid when the situation was dire. Her hesitation was brief before she decided to light the candle. The signal for help did not require the use of spells. The item was imbued with enough magical properties to alert another member of the coven of her distress.

No sooner had she lighted the wick than a guttural noise emanated from the corner of her room. She froze and slowly turned her gaze toward the sound. The bed light in her room lit the dark nook behind her door long enough for her to notice something horrific peering from the shadows. Jensen knocked over the stool to her dresser as she bolted past, and the night-light in her room shattered in the wake of a discordant pitch.

She was already calling Emerson as she stood panting in her living room. She did not know whether her coven leader would show, but the candle had been snuffed out as she had fled the room.

"Hello? Jensen? Is everything o—"

"Emerson! Please come over," she begged. "I need your help. There's something in my house. An entity... I don't know..." She could hardly finish her words. She watched in abject terror as the hall light flickered, and a murkiness washed over the side walls as a shade emerged from the bedroom.

"Get out then! Now. Meet me outside, Jensen. Don't f—" The line crackled and went dead, and the phone seemed to short-circuit. She turned to the front door and tried to yank it open, only to feel a force resist her. She flew around and stood with her back against it as the dark force edged closer.

"Why does the herald to the dead run? Are you not destined to stand against me? I expected more of a *challenge*. Face me, watcher! Or are you weak, like your *mother*?" It spits its insult vehemently. Its voice was the sound of a wind blowing through scorched land. The words came from a long and ashen face with hollow eyes that were birthed from the shadows. The threats deepened and ended in a menacing quake that shook the foundations of her home. "Let me claim your soul so that you may escape the inevitable oblivion that will befall your kind!" it roared. Jensen was pressed against the wall, unable to move in the onslaught of its malice. "I will not be stopped again. Your spirit will perish before the gate can be opened!"

The demon attacked. Lashing out, it tore at her arms as they rose up to cover her face. Its will battered her own into submission. Jensen screamed, but her voice could not penetrate the whirlwind of its fury. She was defenseless. The sound of its infernal voice made her ears ring, and its assault left her numb. Succumbing, she crumpled to the floor, and her hands started to quiver. Then the unexpected happened.

Under the relentless onslaught, a force left her body and pulsed through the ground in a massive shock wave. Hitting the lights that surrounded her, the bulbs sparked to life and started burning with white-hot intensity. The flash of the light made the attacks subside as the demon screeched in pain. It burned in the searing white light until another pulse caused an electrical surge and hammered its ghastly figure against the wall to dissipate into smoke.

Jensen was left shaken by the power that left her body. Everything was quiet. Everything was dark. Nothing moved. Nothing could be felt...except the flow of active magic that coursed through her veins.

6

THE DARK COVENANT

The following morning, Jensen's memory of the previous night trickled back into consciousness. After the attack, she was left disoriented and had hardly processed the banging against her front door. Emerson came crashing through, unaware that the door hadn't been locked. Without the power of the demon forcing it to shut, there was no resistance as his own momentum carried him forward. He had stumbled, and upon seeing Jensen, he fell on the floor beside her to help. Somehow, he had dragged her body to bed, and sleep had come for her, albeit a restless sleep.

She awoke, feeling peculiar. It wasn't only the splitting headache, but a tingling beneath her skin that electrified her senses. There was a shift in her alignment that altered her experience of everything surrounding her. Even the ancient key resting in her pocket weighed differently. It was warm to the touch. She could feel the penetrating vibrations of power coming from it as if its very essence was a part of her. Whatever connection had been made yesterday was now intensified a hundredfold. It left her dazed and confused. In a way, it was as though her body was trying to compensate for its lack of capacity in housing so much power. Yet, none of it could compare to the choir of souls that had begun to assail her mind. Their pleas echoed in her stream of thought, and it was all she could do to block them out.

Emerson sat across from her at the kitchen table, watching as she battled with herself. The concern on his features was evident. He tried masking it behind his normal geniality, but his face was too honest to ever betray his true emotion. He burned to ask her how she was doing but resisted the urge out of respect and realized the obvious; she was rattled.

Reading his mind, she decided to put him out of his misery. "I'll be ok, Emerson. You can ease up now."

The tension of feigned normality deflated, and it was as if she had permitted him to breathe. "*Jesus*, Mills. I leave you for a few hours, and you invite hell to your front door. That is what happened the last time you told me it would be ok." His mouth pulled into the side in a tentative smile that he could not help, despite the evident worry, he must have endured.

She returned the expression. "You've got me there."

There was a rapping on the front door. Emerson jumped at the sudden noise. Frowning, Jensen got up to see who it was. The last face she expected to see as she undid the locks was that of the coven leader. "Greetings, Mills," he sneered. "I—" His words were lost as his face softened in what appeared to be a sudden scholarly analysis of her. Looking her up and down, he commented, "Well, it appears my arrival was providential. Our coven seems to be richer by a fully-realized acolyte. Your powers have manifested. And...I sense you have already cast. Fascinating." Tidus snaked his way past her and stood amid the modest trappings of her apartment.

"Hey, who was...?" Emerson stood in the kitchen entrance, stopping short as he saw the Gate Guardian that had joined Jensen in the living room.

Tidus narrowed his eyes, scrutinizing him. "A legacy. You have the whiff of a soldier on you."

Whatever Emerson was about to say was cut off as he vanished with a snap of the coven leader's fingers. He returned his gaze toward her. "Mills, as a watcher, your fraternization with other covens are to be kept to a minimum. Now, there is no time to lose. It has come to my attention that you and your 'friend' have been busy of late. You will inform me of all that you have discovered while I prepare you for your role among our ranks." The living room melted away from Jensen's sights as Tidus transported them to an undisclosed location before she could even begin to contest or resist him.

THEY WERE at the graveyard where it all started. The coven leader didn't waste any time in submitting her to his relentless string of questioning. After Tidus' interrogation on her impromptu investigation into the crisis faced by the Gate Guardians, including the secrets they had uncovered, the coven leader seemed staunch in his commitment to start training her for what he considered inevitable.

"So, you know of the blood moon. Am I correct?"

"Yes."

"And you know that the alignment of ley energies of that night will permit the fiend behind this fiasco to cast the blood spell. The one that will harvest the souls of witches who have failed to pass over into the hereafter."

"Yes." He was treating her like a schoolchild, and she was rapidly becoming irritated. "Though I'm not sure how our foe seeks to accomplish that."

"Never mind what they seek to do, as we shall seek to stop them. Now that you are a full witch, it will be essential that you harness your unique skill as a gate guardian to prevent the spirit realm from becoming a corral to herd the dead. Now, pay attention to your position." They were in the middle of the graves that had been desecrated four nights before. "You stand at the center of a once-sacred pentacle, warped and tainted through the act of raising five witches from the dead—all of whom were buried in the graves that now lie empty."

"That was why the corpses that attacked our number were as powerful as they had been."

"Correct. Since then, more of the dead were called back. We have managed to put only these new ghouls down and banish the spirits back to the other side. Therefore, your first task will be to reach out to those that now reside in limbo."

"You want me to commune with those malicious spirits that attacked you when they were raised as the undead?"

"The spirits of our brothers and sisters were not malicious but were merely led astray in their motivation. They are in limbo now, confused as to where their souls should wander. *You* must guide them to move on so they may not be recalled into decayed vessels to wreak havoc again."

"You expect much of a witch who has never cast a single spell in her life," she replied, sounding more irritated than she intended.

"I expect much," he said between clenched and grating

teeth, "because your raw power was allegedly enough to drive a demon back to the abyss. No novice could accomplish that! Unfortunately, your mother departed this life so early, as she might have coaxed your powers forth when you were younger, and your training may have started sooner. Only a progenitor can awaken the powers of their seed. Alas, here we are. We have two days left to prepare you. You have no choice but to surrender yourself to the demands of the situation if we are to prevent all that you have seen."

"It is not my fault that the coven has been unresponsive in light of their misguided views on me!" Jensen fired back.

Surprisingly, Tidus didn't react in anger. He simply held up his hand to calm her and indicated that they needed to proceed. "Now, though the spell of reanimation was halted due to the broken tombstone, the ley properties of the incantation still saturates the soil. Open yourself to the spirits and use the traces of what occurred here to find your quarry."

"More than a hundred witches are tormented on the other side, not to mention the thousands of mortals! I cannot just unblock myself."

"You *must*," he commanded. "The key, in your pocket. Use it as an anchor. It will stabilize the voices until the right ones drift your way."

Jensen sighed, knowing she wasn't going to win this one. She took out the skeletal key and tightly wrapped her fingers around it. Jensen concentrated, drawing on its energies, before removing the mental barrier that separated her from the spirit realm. It was like walking into a crowded bazaar, but no longer the head-splitting racket she'd endured this morning. Steadying herself, she focused on keeping her mind severed from any single connection. What she was attempting was not the work of a Gate Guardian;

this was not their domain. It reminded her more of the ways of a necromancer. If she gave in to the pleas of any voice, then she became susceptible to their influence. Instead, she waited. She used the residual clues from the spell that had reanimated the dead. From it, she gleaned the shape of energy that attached itself to the witches that were raised. Among the crowds of spirits, three stood out like lit beacons and grew larger in her vision. "I...see them."

"Good, good. Now, steel yourself. Guide them to the gate and open it for them—*only* for *them*."

The gate in her mind's eye rattled and unlocked, and with her will, she pushed it open. Pandemonium ensued. "The souls, they're all pushing to get through! I—I...cannot hold them back!"

"Do not allow them through! You are not powerful enough to endure the flow of all their power. Resist them. Focus only on the witches!"

She strained against the desires of the desperate dead. Clutching the key harder, she focused and pushed back. The gate was held open by a small crack, wide enough only for the witch's souls to pass through. As their spiritual essences slid through the narrow opening, passing on, she released, and a magnetic force slammed the gate shut. Her knees buckled beneath her, but she did not break contact with the spirit world.

"Mills, you may cease your hold on the gate. I sense they have crossed over."

"I...can't." Jensen watched as the spirits reacted. "There is something else. The dead are angry. Some of them are escaping... They are leaving limbo! Something is drawing them out. I think someone is summoning the dead!"

JENSEN WAS BACK in her apartment, having been told to stay there by the coven leader. Tidus had left to recall the ragtag patrols of Gate Guardians from their separate skirmishes. He would come to collect her then, and the coven would unite their powers in a single concentrated effort to curb the tides of the coming conflict.

Jensen was, however, feeling less and less in favor of her coven's decisions. They had been slow to act. Even without her powers, she had accomplished more than they had over the days that had been lost since the witches had risen. She had begun to think of that violation of nature as a ruse. Perhaps there was significance to it. But it had done nothing but distract the coven from the unfolding plot of their unseen nemesis, so she decided to rebuke her obligations to her superiors and called Emerson.

Setting the arrangement, she met the young detective at a park three blocks away from her home. Since being banished from her apartment by Tidus, he had tried in vain to find out whether Jensen had been alright. Several missed calls and texts greeted her on opening her phone to contact him. No sooner had she reached out than they had devised to elude the watchful eye of her new teacher. Besides their evasive maneuvers, Emerson felt driven to chase the next clue, one which had been right in front of them all along.

They had wound through the decayed streets of the inner city and parked in front of the alley that belonged to the necromancers—the only witches versed well enough in raising the dead. Alison, who had assisted them with the séance, had lost some friends and allies along the way. Friends that were more than happy to sell out the duplicitous bitch when they heard she was wanted by a watcher.

They both stood outside of the car, at the alley's mouth. "You ready?" asked Emerson.

Finding her resolve, Jensen answered, "We were never ready going into this, but we did what we needed to regardless." With that, she was the one to take the first step.

Suspicious characters skulked around every corner. Several fervid glares were thrown their way as they glided cautiously into the grimy pits of that obscure hole. She felt dirty and violated as the attention of renegades, and dark witches focused on her with predatory awareness. Her power was a beacon, and she had not learned to conceal it properly. However, she managed to tap into the Reaper's Key's magical signature and hide it from prying witches' probes. It was safe for the time being, but how safe were they?

"Hey, um, Jensen? Why are you winding to and fro while walking?"

Emerson's question was odd. The alley was packed with witches passing them on every side. Surely he would be dodging them as much as she was. "There is a lot of traffic down here. I don't want to bump into anyone and attract attention," she whispered.

Emerson went pale. "But...there is no one down here. It's just us."

Jensen went stiff. Looking around her, she realized how inattentive she was to the absence of footfalls and the in corporeality of the shapes that passed them. They were not walking among a leering assortment of necromancers. They were wandering among the dead. "Emerson, there are spirits. All around us," she said anxiously. "I—"

Emerson touched her arm and whispered urgently. "Ignore them. Don't try to connect or reach out. Don't send them back. Not here. Not now. Let's get to the bottom of this first."

She swallowed hard, nodding in agreement, and then

kept walking. Emerson hovered closer, even offering to take the lead as they came to the end of the alley. He didn't know what she saw, but he was willing to shield her from whatever it was. He felt a disturbance in the air, as well. When he suddenly stopped, Jensen was almost convinced that the spirits had manifested stronger. Enabling him to see them, but looking over his shoulder quickly made her discount the theory.

"Alison." Her name was ground through Emerson's teeth, and he made no effort to conceal his contempt.

The raven-haired necromancer stood in front of them, flanked by two other witches. The smile that Jensen once thought mischievous now only seemed despicable. "You made a mistake bringing her here, Emerson. You cannot stop what is coming."

"You used us to gain an edge. I called you an ally once," he hissed.

"Alliances change when the scale does not weigh in your favor. It is because of *them*, our world is in jeopardy," she announced, pointing at Jensen. "They deny the return of our fallen brethren. They call themselves the judicators of death, yet do not even permit themselves to listen to the voices of the defendants."

"You are being toyed with!" Jensen exclaimed. "You accept the desires of the dead in all their misgivings, even when they speak no reason. Even when their actions on the other side are not prescribed by their own will!"

"Lies! You are the villains here, Gate Guardian. You are not fit to hold the key to the gates. You will come to feel the wrath of those you have tried to force through!" As her last words fell, the ghosts that had spared them either some or no attention turned on them.

"Emerson...get behind me. Now!"

The jaws of the specters surrounding them fell open, and nightmarish wails escaped into the night. The spirits converged in the attack.

Plunging her hand in her pocket, the Reaper's Key slid into her palm. She mouthed words she had never learned, allowing her power to pour into it, and through it directed her will to halt the spirits where they stood. Time stood still, and she didn't even realize her eyes had closed in anticipation of the assault. A wraithlike nexus swirled around them as the souls were siphoned into the key, and she could feel how the witches crossed back through into the spirit world.

The necromancers who had shackled the witch spirits to do their bidding now seemed hesitant as they faced them. Alison looked both stupefied and angry as she realized their plan had backfired. Making use of the upper hand that had presented itself, Jensen drew on the magical residue of their failed incantation to shape a counter spell. The magic rebounded. With it, she fused their own souls to their flesh, taking away how they could express their spiritual essence through magic. Focusing it even more through the artifact, she took control of the contained energies inside their bodies and forced them to their knees. Groaning in agony, the necromancers succumbed to her power.

"Your actions here tonight are abominable. Talk, you scum! Or shall I make your lips move?" Jensen's eyes were wild, and even Emerson seemed taken aback by the anger in her voice. "Who is responsible for this? The raising of the dead, the vandalization of the guardian's tomb, the summoning of the demon... *Who?*" Jensen didn't know if she imagined it, but she swore that she saw Alison flinch in disbelief at the mention of the demon. The reaction did not last long. The key pulsed with poisonous green light as the toxicity of suppressed magic within the necromancers' cells made them writhe in agony.

"Argh! Desist, I beg you, please! It was a woman...a member of the coven," the man to Alison's right shouted. "A powerful caster!" he exclaimed painfully between gasping breaths. "She is responsible for the Gravetide spell that reanimated the remains from the dead...there is a demon bound to—"

"Fool!" Alison heaved. "Be quiet! We would *never* align with a—" She uttered a scream of pain as the magic burned in her blood.

Jensen intensified the spell. She wasn't sure how she was accomplishing the feat, but it was as if she was flexing muscles that she only now remembered to use. "You have no choice but to speak! Do you understand? The Gravetide spell. Tell me what it is. Why was it cast?"

The other necromancer tried to answer in a ragged breath. She did not make eye contact. "To allow the casting of the Gravetide spell! It will...tie the energies of the departed to our own. When they pass on, their magic won't be lost. It will pass onto those left behind, those of us that must continue their work. You cannot stop the spell! If you do, the souls that have crossed back over will be forced to haunt the earth forever!"

The man, terrified, spoke up once more. "There is more. It—"

Alison jumped at her companion, attempting to halt his betrayal. Still, on Jensen's whim, the sharp pang of magic stopped her.

"It seals a dark covenant!" he continued. "When the souls of five witches are taken, the gates of the hereafter close. It prevents the departed to move on... Their souls will be stolen from limbo and converted to the newly damned on earth through the Gravetide spell. Please! Have mercy!"

Jensen didn't feel merciful. Their stories were too conflicting. She didn't know what to believe. A rage had overtaken her that she found difficult to shake. She felt a hand land lightly on her shoulder and turned to see the cheerful luster stolen from Emerson Allen's eyes, replaced by a wordless plea for her to stop—and so, she did.

The relentless pressure that held the witches subsided, though she did not release her hold. They sagged to the floor, completely spent by their fight against their own magic.

Alison spoke first. "Your efforts will be in vain," she spat. "We are not misguided here. You are. The Gravetide spell will preserve us. It will bond us with our ancestors; allow them to return when we need them. They will make this world theirs and set themselves atop pedestals from which to guide our actions. Your kind is destroying us! Making us weaker!"

The necromancer was a fanatic. She was genuinely convinced that it would save their kind. A consistent truth, however, became apparent. "The risen dead had a purpose," Emerson whispered to Jensen. "The greater scheme was already set in motion four days ago. The Gravetide spell had upset the spirit world by twisting the souls of five witches so they could be placed in the reanimated corpses from the cemetery. If what this guy said is true, then the tainted pentacle could be the sign-off to a deal with hell, and the demon was the mediator to ensure that it was carried out. However, I don't think all of them even know the demon is involved."

"Then the Gate Guardians were kept preoccupied," Jensen continued, "in dealing with the monsters that had been risen; it was a misjudgment that worked in the enemy's favor. Meanwhile, it had possibly set the stage for a far greater atrocity synchronized to the upcoming blood moon." She almost didn't recognize the eloquence by which she deduced the pattern. "The Gravetide spell had sealed the gates to the hereafter and left the spirits on the other side stranded for either a harvest or a slaughter. Maybe they would simply return of their own accord. Yet, the involvement of infernal forces meant that their return would not bode well for the living—despite the necromancers' ideals."

Like the snap of an elastic, the bonds to Jensen's trapping enchantment were severed. It jolted her, and she looked in alarm as the necromancers sensed their freedom and spirited away. It happened faster than either she or Emerson could process.

"Dammit!" she uttered.

"Now, now, there's no need to be upset." A woman emerged from the shadows. "It's just a game, is it not? You have played with the children. Now, their mother has come to supervise."

7

MOTHER OF DARKNESS

"Tell your detective to leave, dear. We cannot have a good chat with the muscle listening in on us," the woman said lazily, regarding Emerson with passive disdain.

"I am not going anywhere," he answered bravely.

Jensen studied the new arrival. Her porcelain features were completely unravaged by the mark of either age or joy, kept smooth by the glacial contempt she held toward others. To Jensen, she appeared like a wild tempest personified, with black hair exploding in wild rivulets all around her face like a dark mane, streaked with the flash of silver. She surmised quickly that the woman was not about to waste time on the triviality of compromise. With a heavy conscience, she turned to her friend and looked him in the eye. "Emerson—"

"No! Jensen, I'm not leaving. I don't trust her!"

"Neither do I," Jensen agreed without attempting to hide her voice, "but we don't have much time. Let me speak to her. We need to get closer to the truth before it's too late."

Emerson pursed his lips and tensed his jaw, trying to

hold back his frustration. Jensen felt for him. He was always being excluded. Always being pushed aside, and yet he had been the fulcrum upon which they had devised their answers to the swelling mystery. He looked from one woman to the other, and then nodded. Turning on his heel, he whispered, "Call me when you need me," in an almost detached manner. Then, he walked away.

When he was out of earshot, the woman was the first to speak. "You are quite the fiery neophyte, aren't you? It's extraordinary—to have bloomed so late, yet so beautifully. If only your potential wasn't bound by the delusion of your coven."

"What do you know of my coven, or even what I am capable of? More importantly, who the hell are you to make such claims?"

"Elsie Turner. Trust me when I tell you that your coven knows exactly who I am. Their actions are not unknown to any of us. I am aware of the saga variables and who holds the power as opposed to those who are influenced. You won't stop us, Jensen Mills, even though I sense your fervent desire to do so. The blood spell will be cast, and with it, I will reclaim what is lost. I will reclaim what has been wrongfully taken from me."

"Your entitlement to power will be the end of you—of all of our kind! You don't know what you are doing, Elsie."

"Power?" she scoffed. "You think I am driven by power? I do not care for the little magic of other witches. My intentions are fueled solely in restoring my family...massacred before they were granted the opportunity to reshape the world upon which our culture is built."

"Why do *all* of this then? Why not just bring back your family?"

Elsie laughed hysterically. "A reanimation of *that* kind of power, only to trap them in the rotting vessels left behind in this world? I think not. Their physical forms will only limit them. Years in limbo have honed their craft. They have waited for their chance in the spirit world, escaping the tireless vigil of the Gate Guardians. The veil shall be lifted, and they will step back into this world in spirit alone, more powerful than ever before."

"To what end? Vengeance? Why not just track down those responsible for their death?"

"The coward whose hands run with their blood eludes even them, but it does not matter. If anything, the wretch did them a favor. If any vengeance is to be exacted, it will be on the Watchers who prevented their return. Their misguided duty starves the witching world of the knowledge of our ancestors. When we cast down the prison that you guard, all the dead will walk the earth. We will seize secrets lost to us by allowing their keepers to return."

Jensen thought the woman was mad. She was driven insane by a victory she had not claimed. She might not realize she was being used by powers far greater than herself. "You are the delusional one! You are being used. You have invited forces into this that you cannot even begin to understand. I will not allow you to succeed..."

"You, a fledgling witch? You boast promises that will be your undoing. I am the one who holds all the cards."

"And you have built a house from it that will topple. What about your demon, hmm? Do you really think he is just some lackey in your plan? Who serves who, *Elsie*?" she taunted.

Elsie cocked her head to the side, almost amused by Jensen's nerve to challenge her. "Some find backdoor detectives to mope around on the sidelines, while others ensure their efforts by taking hell into their employ. I have dealt with demons before. This one shall be no different when the work is complete."

Jensen thought back on the attack in her apartment. The demon had nearly torn her and her psyche apart. In fact, had it not been toying with her, she may have been dead sooner. The blast of her awakened power had driven the demon away and left her spent. She could not imagine the amount of energy needed to actually control it. "Then I will stand ready to kick your hellhound to the curb."

"Ha! You lack the knowledge, the skill, and the refinement of your craft that comes with years of practice. You warded off the demon by sheer luck alone, and your little stunt a moment ago against the necromancers was fed solely by emotional expression. You have yet to scratch the surface of your power, and you presume to stop a plan that you have only begun to understand? Don't make me laugh." Her tone was contemptuous and overconfident but nonetheless effective in making Jensen doubt herself. Elsie was right; she might be fighting a battle on her terms, but she was fighting it alone.

"You will not dissuade me from trying!"

"You are a plucky little fool, aren't you? You should be groveling, you little ingrate. I am giving you a chance to discard this preposterous bravado and step down. The time of the Gate Guardians is at an end. You are in a losing race against the inevitable. I suggest you leave to find solace in the mundane."

Jensen felt furious, but she was smart enough to know that you could not speak reason with insanity. She backed away, holding the look that was exchanged between the two women. In that breadth of silence, both saw that the other was not about to give up. *This is not over*, she thought, making sure that intention was communicated through her eyes. She turned and left.

As she ran back along the alley, Alison returned, flanked by more necromancers. Her eyes followed as the Gate Guardian bolted down the narrow passage. Looking up, she saw more of her number peeking through the lattices of apartment windows. With a curt nod, the necromancers, aware of the retreating Gate Guardian, set off in pursuit.

Jensen was running. The entire alley unsettled her, and she had no idea what lurked behind the doors and drawn curtains she rushed past. She was sure there were unseen eyes that followed her every move. Dark energy wafted from every brick of the buildings that towered to her sides. She suspected that the necromancers were far more in number than any of her covens had envisioned. It was all she could do to compose herself when one jumped out in front of her, blocking her way out.

She could hear the rapid approach of footsteps as more of them came up behind her. They seemed to crawl out from everywhere then. Coming out of doors, hanging from window sills, jumping from metal staircases, and emerging from behind crates, stalls, and other loose miscellaneous objects that lay strewn down the alley. She was surrounded.

"What have you done, bitch?" one man snarled between the rungs of the stairs.

"The dead have gone silent! What injustice have your kind committed now?" another asked.

A woman pushed her from the front, and she caught her footing before she stumbled. "You entitled little whelp! Undo what you have done."

"I have no idea what you are talking about!" Jensen challenged back.

"I think you do," she heard as a familiar voice drifted

from the background. "I think you have played the innocent for a long time now, *guardian*."

"Our connections to the dead have been severed," another necromancer said—the same one who had tried to weave a deception earlier. "We have tried raising our brethren, contacting them, but to no avail! This is your doing!"

Jensen frowned. She didn't know what was happening. They were confronting her for being unable to channel their dark sorcery, unable to perform the abominable things that were in violation of the natural law. She took small comfort in the fact that they could take command of a horde of spirits to assault her. Still, there was plenty that a bunch of able-bodied witches could do to her on a physical level.

"Undo it! *Now!*" another man growled from behind. "Or we shall make you." They moved, closing in on her like a ring of sharks. Their faces were contorted in something more than anger or frustration. It was as if they had been deprived of something they needed, as if everything was a mindless action-driven on by the madness that comes with withdrawal.

"You all need help. You're addicted to the powers of the dead..."

"Enough!" The converging necromancers froze in place at the command, trying to control their trembling bodies. She could see a few of them struggle...itching to move in and close their hands around her throat. Jensen could put up a fight. She was tall, athletic, and knew a thing or two about defending herself. However, she had never fought hand to hand with a cluster of deprived death magic junkies.

The necromancers parted, and Elsie emerged again. The haughtiness had been wiped from her face and was now replaced by a marked of disapproval. "What is the meaning of this? You chase young girls while there is a rival coven that needs to be reckoned with."

"Pardon mistress," the man who had groveled in their earlier confrontation began, "but we are unable to use our death magic to summon or raise the dead. We cannot call on their aid. Without their spiritual force-feeding our spells, we cannot hope to overwhelm the watchers. The other side meets us with silence."

"It is *her* fault!" Alison hissed. "She must pay! We must—"

"Hush!" Elsie snapped. She closed her eyes in concentration. Jensen immediately knew what she was doing. She could feel the tendrils of Elsie's consciousness, reaching out into the spirit realm. She wasn't sure how she could sense her thoughts prodding around the dead stuck in limbo. She wondered if the Reaper's Key had bestowed her with the ability. Her magic traces were vague, which was strange, considering how powerful she sensed Elsie to be. Still, it pierced through the veil and found its target. She was reaching out to one soul, then many, all of whose magic felt similar to her own. As the witches in the alley were baited by their 'mother' call for a ceasefire, Jensen was sure that Elsie communicated with the very witches she sought to bring back. Her eyes opened, and she directed a glare in Jensen's direction.

"Well, upstart, it appears that you have meddled yet again." Jensen suddenly felt burdened by the weight of a hundred accusing eyes, but she kept eye contact with Elsie alone. She returned the gate guardian's look, but in a resonant voice that was both deceptive and charismatic, Elsie addressed her following of necromancers that flooded the alley. "The young witch has prematurely begun to seal the gates."

A muffled collection of insults and angry reactions met Jensen's ears. "What are you talking about?" she asked. "The gate in the spirit world is sealed by your doing. You cannot blame me for your own transgressions."

"I am not talking of the gate that leads to the hereafter," Elsie responded, with poison lacing each word. "You have begun to shut the gates through which the deceased pass from this world into the valley of souls."

Jensen's eyes widened. *There was another gate? Could she seal that as well?* The questions hammered against her skull as she tried to focus on the present danger. The witches around her were not responding kindly to the news and started to get keyed up on reacting by their dark instincts.

"The Gate Guardian has committed the ultimate insult by which her people are guilty: She has locked us out of the realm of the departed. She is their new champion, the newly born gate guardian. Her powers have manifested and now threaten to unravel the very fabric of our efforts. Children! We cannot stand by and watch as the foundations of our power are cut off from us." The malicious grin that passed over her face made Jensen shudder as the next command left her lips. "Take the girl. Bind her, and let us teach a valuable lesson to the imbecilic bravery of green witches."

They nearly sprawled over one another to get to her. Rough hands grabbed her by the scruff of her jacket and yanked her down to the cold floor. Then a gunshot fired, and the necromancers around her dispersed in alarm, looking down toward the alley mouth. Emerson stood there with his gun pointed to the sky. It was a reckless move, considering how outnumbered they were. Still, it had distracted them long enough for Jensen to focus herself on enacting a defense.

Augmenting her spell with the key, she sent a shock

wave through the alleyway. The force disembodied the spirits of the necromancers, knocking them right from their bodies. Unconscious, their vessels fell. Jensen bashed through the bodies that barricaded her from the end of the alley. The effect was only temporary. No sooner had she started to run than the untethered spirits returned to their material forms and began to awaken again. She cleared the last necromancer by a single bound and rushed to lessen the space that separated her from the detective.

"*Nooo,*" she heard Elsie scream. She had clearly not been affected by the magical attack. Jensen could hear as she barked enraged commands to her coven, which was coming back to their senses. By that point, she reached Emerson, who grabbed her by the arm and led her out of the alley.

"Emerson! You crazy bastard! You never left!"

His eyes were almost feral with the adrenaline. Still, a smile blazed across his face before he looked over her shoulder to see the necromancers advancing. "I couldn't let you have all the fun! But look, we aren't out of the dog box. That bitch has just set her entire pack on us. We need to get out of here..."

"You don't have to tell me twice," Jensen stated between panting breaths. Emerson's car was still parked where he had left it when bringing them to the alley. Jumping in, they sped off. Her eyes were fixed on the rearview mirror, watching as the necromancers flooded into the street like an army of ants pouring forth from their nest.

8

THE CROSSROADS OF POWER

T his time, Emerson took them to his place for the night. *God, Mills*, she thought, *you really need to stop being so comfortable with people you just met.* Exhaustion afforded her little deliberation, though. Gentleman as he was, Emerson had taken the couch, offering Jensen his bed. It was an offer she kindly refused and an argument she eventually won to force him to sleep in his own room. He had already proven that chivalry was alive and well. He was allowed a moment of selfishness, even though it was hard for him. Whatever reconnaissance and recollection they had planned on that night was firmly pushed out to the next day.

The next morning, Jensen looked like a hot mess. The mirror was cruel in revealing its truths. Her auburn hair was like a forest fire. Her eyes a cradle to all her problems and she found herself staring at this lanky disheveled thing that had failed to pull off the appearance of a fully realized Wiccan goddess. She wondered how the divine solved their problems and why they weren't involved in deciding the spirit world's fate.

Things had escalated pretty quickly since her powers awakened. To add, in the last few days, she had discovered more truths than she had ever come to know compared to the previous decade of her life. There was more depth to the rivalry her coven was involved in with their dark counter-parts: The necromancers. Apparently, hell was more acces-sible than she had imagined, and demons could be summoned like duplicitous watchdogs to oversee the unfolding of a plan. Did the other necromancers know Elsie was messing around with such forces? It was risky to carry around keys that could unlock dormant powers, mob violence, and the spirit gates. Above all, dying seemed to be quite a hassle when there was always another gateway you needed to pass through.

"You have many choices to make, don't you?" she asked her reflection. She didn't need an answer. Her eyes were filled with resignation. Sighing, she took a shower, and after getting dressed, she found Emerson in the kitchen. A full spread of breakfast options awaited her, complete with a table fully set. "Oh my God, you did all this?"

"Yup! Please have a seat. I bet you that you could use it after yesterday. Besides, since starting this 'adventure,' I can't remember us really eating much, to be honest."

She realized he was right. They had been functioning on adrenaline and possibly caffeine alone. "Come to think of it, I am starving. As if we didn't have enough to swallow down."

"Damn straight. So, help yourself. No use plotting vigi-lante witch excursions on an empty stomach."

She hesitated in starting. "Maybe I should just scoff this down. We probably should get going to do whatever the hell we need to stop all this."

"Listen, Mills, there is time. Eat something first, and let's play around with what we know." They did just that. Both of them were well into their meals before Emerson started prodding between sips of coffee. "Why don't you start by telling me what this...*Elsie*...told you?"

"You know her name?"

"You pick up a few of them when you're a legacy that cannot tap into your magic and has nothing better to do but snoop around."

"Emerson, in all seriousness, we would not have the advantages we do if it wasn't for you." She hoped her compliment came across sincerely. When he had been forcibly excused from the conversation with the necromancer, Jensen had sworn he became tired of playing the sidekick.

There was a glimmer of understanding in those eyes. For the first time, his smile was less successful at hiding an almost disconsolate undertone. She was sure he had a hard time in the throes of his own uncertainty about his past. Meanwhile, he was very accommodating at being available to solve the mysteries of *her* world. For that reason, she started sharing everything she knew.

"Elsie intends to bring back her family. She believes them to be some pagan messiahs that will come to reshape the world of our craft. However, she doesn't intend to reanimate them. In performing the Gravetide spell, the veils between our worlds will drop, and they will simply pass back through, fully incorporeal. As ghosts, their magic will be a hundred times more powerful than when it would have been when bound by flesh."

Emerson's brow furrowed in answer, "But, the blood spell...the monk believed that it would mass harvest the energies of the witches trapped on the other side. That their spirits would wither away. Wouldn't she destroy her family?"

"It may be that his account was an old one, or one of the

conflicting lies that has been told over the years. You heard the necromancers yesterday when I enacted my spell of bonding on them. The woman tried to deceive us. I doubt that her blind loyalty would have shifted under torture. The man, however, seemed to fold under pressure, and fear may have forced an answer out of him."

"I, um..." He was tentative. "I've meant to ask you about that. Jensen, what was that all about?"

She knew what he was referring to. Her sudden bout of rage had surprised even her. She looked down at her reflection on the surface of coffee in her cup, an almost iconic representation to accompany the musings of her dark side. "I don't know. I think that, since coming into my magic, I've been feeling different. Not just more capable, but also more intense. It is like everything I experience or feel has been magnified. Maybe the pressure got to me. The ownership of this key and the weight it places on my shoulders are great. Now, I think I'm at the crossroads of making a difficult decision...and I sometimes wonder what my mother would have done. What would she have said to me right now?"

There was sympathy in Emerson's eyes. She thought he understood better than most people. He might have longed for the guidance of his parents as well. "What are the choices before you?"

Jensen sat back in her chair, looking up at the ceiling, gathering her thoughts. Then she answered, "There is more than one gate to limbo. One leads to the hereafter. It was the gate closed by the Gravetide spell four days ago—the one I have been trying to pry open so that the souls can move on. But there is another gate that leads into the realm of the dead from our world. The necromancers came for me because I had started to shut the second without knowing. I think that happened when the spirits that almost attacked us were drawn through the Reaper's Key to be placed back in limbo. It must have nearly closed it because so many souls were moving through."

"So, you need to decide..."

"...whether this gate stays open, or whether I should shut it forever."

The air around them sparked to life, and from the ether, a maelstrom of paper descended over them and settled in disorganized heaps on the kitchen floor. They were the guardian scrolls she and Emerson had taken to the friar, mixed with the torn pages from other ancient texts. A few seconds later, an envelope materialized and drifted down until Emerson grabbed at it. Looking at the seal, his curiosity warped into apprehension. "It's from Friar Ambrose."

"He must have translated the text. That was pretty coincidental if you ask me. This is quite a way to get some feedback. Who needs email, right?" she joked.

"Yeah..." he said, his hand trembling ever so slightly. After staring at it another two seconds, he went about to open it. Inside was a long letter, nearly filled to the very margins with the scribbles of the monk. Emerson's eyes darted back and forth as he read. Jensen forced herself to be patient, even though anticipation was gnawing at her senses. She was caressing the key in her pocket. In the span of the last few days, it had almost become a comforting charm that she had grown accustomed to. *Sure*, she had told herself, *it was a bit macabre that it was a finger bone fashioned into a witch's trinket, but other people kept shells in their pocket. Skeletons have long been romanticized.*

"Oh my God. Jensen, you have to read this." He handed the letter to her and immediately dove into the heaps of paper that surrounded them. Friar Ambrose's handwriting started off neatly enough. Still, as the letter progressed, she could see how he had written with more haste. The letters became violent strokes and dashes that seemed to trail off in bits as though he had been interrupted. There was a disquietude in looking at that letter, and she felt that they had unwittingly put one of their own in danger.

MILLS,

I hope the contents of this letter reach you in good stead. You may be needed now more than ever. Our time is short, and the task that lies ahead of you is monumental.

I was mistaken. My perusal of the guardian's scrolls has revealed secrets that threaten far more than our own people in this saga that has developed. I do not know who lies behind the unfolding atrocities, but they cannot be permitted to succeed.

At the rise of the blood moon, the Gravetide spell will be cast, ripping the veil that hangs between the mortals' realms and that of the spirits. The dead will return, some manic from their time spent in wait, and with them, they will bring the magic untethered to mortal flesh. They will not be the only ones to return. With them will come their tormentors—other forces locked away in the realm of spirits, unable to pass the barrier of the magical veil.

When the blood moon wanes, horror will be descended unto the earth. The veil will be torn, and the gates will shut, leaving the departed to wander this earth—forever...

Without the means to pass on, the spirits will be driven insane by the dark forces that cross over from the other side. In their crazed vindictiveness, they will launch attacks on the living. Possessing them, inflicting harm on their children, killing mercilessly, and drowning the world in the havoc that ensues. Hell will rise from the bowels of the earth to its surface.

. . .

THE BLOOD SPELL must be stopped! You must seal the gate from both ends—empty limbo of its occupants. Seal the gate from both ends. Lock the monstrosities of purgatory in their cages forever. You must become the anchor by which the souls who remain in this world will be kept in check.

The mistakes of the past must be rewritten...

JENSEN PUT DOWN THE LETTER. "The mistakes of the past...?"

"This has happened before," Emerson answered, raising some of the notes and the accompanying ancient texts. "Jensen, some of these stories predates even the Dark Ages. Some claim that a spell may have even been instrumental in causing it."

"He keeps referring to other nightmares as well. Also, he mentioned limbo...purgatory. Christian traditions believed it was an in-between place where souls experience a final cleansing by fire before they were allowed to move on. Is that why the souls grow restless when they are unable to do so? They are stuck in there with...something...that torments them?"

"Wait, I saw something here. Ah, here we go." He fanned out illustrated texts that depicted creatures of myth. Fae, goblins, djinn, and other mythical beasts of legend that she couldn't even begin to recognize. Whatever romantic notions people may have attached to them was lost on the Gate Guardians. The Fae were depicted as succubi that seduced mortals with their deceptive beauty. Some mythical creatures' majesty seemed twisted and wrong. They were painted as vicious monstrosities that tore in flesh and spirit. Pages upon archival scripts' pages displayed horrific images of purgatory, and a hurried look over some of the translations affirmed her worst fears.

"Dammit," Jensen exclaimed, "this just became so much more fucking complex than we ever imagined."

Emerson was still gathering up and organizing some notes. He was only half listening as more of the information caught his eye. "And here...this talks of how multiple covens had to unite when the terrors were released on earth. The veil dropped, allowing the dead...and other things...to pass through. Then the gates sealed, preventing anyone, or anything, from passing either on or back. It initiated a time of chaos and a war that lasted years to ward off evil. It says here that the covenant of the Gate Guardians was sealed during this time. Death magic changed forever, and the darker traditions were abolished."

Jensen paced around the kitchen, mulling over the striking truths that now lay revealed around them. "What about the gate guardians? There must be something about them there. What was their explicit role? Were they the ones to find a solution? They must have reopened the gates, banished the abysmal monsters back to purgatory, and regulated the passing of witch and mortal spirits."

Emerson looked around him. He picked up one paper, then a second from a different pile, and finally a third. Quick cursory glances at the gist of the information made his eyes go wide with a mix of angst and excitement. "They did, but their role was secretive. Fascinating..." He read in silence for a few seconds before his boyhood curiosity started to make Jensen too tense.

"Uh, Emerson... Feel free to share anytime, please. We might just be able to stop an apocalypse tomorrow."

"Oh, man. I'm sorry. Damn, Mills, what your ancestors did..."

"Please, enlighten me."

"It says here that the only magic that could undo the consequences of a blood spell was more blood magic. But they didn't have a blood moon to rely on. Hence, they used death magic according to their own devices. Your ancestors were a rebellious group of Gate Guardians who went against the explicit wishes of their brethren. Their blood spell had to be more powerful to negate the violent magic of the trapped spirits and nether beasts from purgatory. Without celestial energy to magnify their efforts, they needed to find another way to compensate—to summon enough magic. The only way...was a sacrifice."

"Friar Ambrose hinted at the notion of sacrifice once. What did they have to give up?"

"Their lives."

"*What?*" She was shocked. The move seemed excessive. It almost emulated fanatic devotion.

"To fashion a key. The Reaper's Key. This spell, the one to counter the blood spell cast years before, would require more than just blood. Four would give their lives, while a fifth would become the conduit. It required them to shape an artifact from their very body, belonging to one of their own. With it, they could seal the gate, banish the monsters, herd the souls back to limbo, and leave open the gates so that the departed may never be prevented from crossing over."

Jensen thought back on the confrontation in the alley and how she had pulled the souls that unrightfully waded on earth back through the key. "All this talk of harvesting souls," she realized, "it was misunderstood. I think I know why they called this the Reaper's Key. It was the 'sickle' by which the dead were harvested back into the spirit realm."

"That is why our lives are in peril. Once they realize you

had the one thing to undo their work, they would come for you. They would account for all contingencies."

"Friar Ambrose had it wrong then," Jensen said, frustrated. "His hunches and suspicions were a misdirection in itself, even though he may not have intended it. They would never be able to use the key to cast the spell. They needed to prevent it from being used to stop them."

"Not all of it. Think about it. Witchkind, in maintaining the natural order, would always stand in the way of dark forces unleashing chaos in the world. When souls in limbo don't pass on, their energies are never revived in the mortal realm when new witches are born. Those who were destined to be witches are born without power, and fewer and fewer witches are left to stand against the monsters." Emerson tangled his hand in his hair, feeling drained as the realizations fell one by one like a line of dominoes.

"There is still a glaring problem with all of this... All this knowledge relates to how the damage done by a blood spell was overturned by another. Still, nothing here mentions how to actually stop it. Also, which faction cast the *true* Gravetide spell? There are too many plot holes. We cannot just sit around waiting for them to wreak havoc and then come in as the cleaning squad. Besides, I wouldn't know how to even begin herding back thousands of souls, much less banish mythical creatures."

Emerson took a deep breath before asking, "So, the gate then. What do you think must be done?"

Jensen looked him in the eye, long and hard, before answering. "Well, Detective, I think it's better to leave a door open instead of wondering what lies behind it. I won't close the gate."

Emerson smiled. "What will you do instead?"

She groaned. "I think it's time to face the music and reestablish contact with my coven."

"YOU IMPUDENT LITTLE BITCH! You dare display such audacity among us?" Lenora screeched.

The shock on Summer's Taylor's usually composed face was almost comical as her equal lashed out temperamentally toward her niece. Summer wasn't fairly sure what to make of her news either, but she was the only one whose reaction was anywhere near remotely calm compared to the rest. Next to Lenora, Desmond—her companion—mirrored her expression of scorn.

"Forgive me, Lenora, but as the only one to command the power to execute the needed course of action, I will be as audacious as I please. So please bite your tongue. Bite it off, in fact, before you forget your gentility in front of your new recruits again."

That did it, Jensen thought. Lenora was absolutely seething at this point.

"Mills! You will respect a senior Watcher. Do you understand me? To a degree, I share Lenora's sentiment. You dare much by showing your face without acknowledging your disobedience, while simply strolling in and claiming the right to make decisions that will affect our world." Tidus was surprisingly diplomatic while being firm. Jensen knew that he knew her talents were valuable. He would not lose his temper like the other coven member did, for fear of losing her allegiance. The entire coven of Gate Guardians had gathered in the mortuary. All of their acolytes had been summoned: The elders, the masters, their militia, and their initiates. She was enduring the obloquy of every eye that was fixed on her.

She wasn't sure whether it had much to do with her forceful entry in the middle of their held council or the fact that they could not deny her claim because of the very powers they knew she had come to possess. "Pardon me, *master*," she began with emphasized derision, "but it is your obsessive obligation to manners and status that has perhaps been the greatest bane to our cause. I will *not* show respect to a member who has shunned me before I have even begun to show my worth." Her eyes blazed with fire as she stared Lenora down, melting the woman's glacial defenses as the cold bitch that she was. "Your condemnation of me, based purely off of my mother's actions, was juvenile. I begin to understand why she may have done things to deliberately upset this coven."

You could hear a pin drop in the room. She was treading on thin ice, but time was of the essence. There was no use walking on eggshells as well.

"Mills..." Tidus gritted his teeth, assuming a tone of warning.

She couldn't fathom how a scholarly group could be preoccupied with 'tradition' after all that she had just related. She had told them everything, and still, they chose ridicule over action. This could not be what was left from those first Gate Guardians who had zealously met the apocalyptic world centuries ago. She believed that they might still be convinced that the events foreseen were not to happen at all.

"Enough. Listen to me! We have one day. *One* single day to meet this crisis. The dead will return, the veil will fall, and hell will rise. There is no more time for deliberation. You must act!"

This time, Desmond lost his cool. "You forget yourself! It is preposterous. A young witch ordering her coven to act on her whims. It—"

He nearly choked on the words he retained as Tidus raised his hand to quiet his equal. It was the most surprising thing he had ever done, in her opinion. He looked at Jensen with something very different from the scathing looks he often reserved for her. This time, those old eyes held a steely challenge. "If we were to act, what would you propose we do?"

Jensen didn't need to think long. It was impulsive, but perhaps even ridiculous enough to succeed. "Attack. To attack their coven while they are trying to restore their connection to the spirit realm. I managed to close the gate to limbo only slightly, but it was enough to cut them off from their abilities. They could no longer speak to the dead or call their specters to haunt this plane. Perhaps I could do it again, just hold it ajar ever so slightly. Only temporarily. After we win, I'll fling it back open. Without their spiritual ties, they become reckless in the wake of their withdrawal. To them, their twisted death magic is like a drug. They'll be vulnerable. The time is perfect. We need to do this before they regain enough energy to bring back more of the dead. You know what damage has been done. Some of our ranks have already fallen or been taken. Nothing prevents them from raising more of those broken bodies to do their gruesome work in fending you off."

"We do not attack a coven unless directly provoked," another elder answered.

"And this is *not* direct provocation? This is madness. They seek to make your time end. They regard you as the prejudiced jailers of the departed. If they succeed with this spell, they will come for you first."

"Which is why the dead are our main concern, and our efforts should be directed at the realm of the dead and making it inaccessible to the necromancers. One part of your plan holds merit—to close the gate—but it will not be a mere ruse to leave us with the deranged and addicted. You will shut the gate completely." Tidus had assumed the neutral tone that the Watchers had become famous for.

Jensen felt like she was talking to a brick wall. Her jaw hung slack as the words escaped her in how she could respond. In the end, she found herself capable of but a single word. "No."

Tidus's eyebrow rose. Muffled exchanges happened among the other members as a tension swooped through them. "You refuse a direct order from your leader."

"When it is delusional, yes. What you are proposing is sealing the souls of those who die on this earth. It will leave the spirits crazed as they crave release. We will create a paranormal confinement that will be too much for us to control."

Summer, her aunt, stepped forward. Her address toward her niece was far milder and more pleading. "Jensen, please. We need you to see reason. We will deal with the dead as they become a nuisance on this plane. We will find another way by which they can return."

"With your ability to seal the gate, we will guard against the necromancers from ever using their ability to affect the dead adversely again. Our first duty—our main duty—is to guard the dead. We will do so wherever they dwell. Our actions here tonight will preserve peace among the spirits for generations. If the dead should act by their own accords and seek to meddle in the affairs of mortals, we shall rein them in."

"They are not to be herded!" Jensen exclaimed. "What

difference lies between you and Elsie's coven if you regard the spirits as nothing more than cattle to be managed?"

"The deceased see no reason! Some souls are incapable of overcoming the trepidations of death. Do not flatter yourself in claiming to understand their devices and intentions. The necromancers did the same, and through it, they were misled into doing the bidding of spirits. It has driven them mad and made them addicted to the magic that they draw on. They have been promised more power than they have been capable of dealing with for centuries." The coven leader was starting to realign himself with the anger and condemnation he reserved for those who opposed him. "Now, you will shut the gate to the other side. Indefinitely. Your act shall be irreversible. Then, we will strike and make sure the necromancers become no threat." The coven mumbled and reacted in approval while watching and waiting, as Jensen's face contorted under the weight of the choice—or rather, the command.

Jensen began to think that she should have never suggested the idea. Tidus had forced it to the pole of the extreme and now sought to take chances under the pressure of the looming crisis. "I won't do it." She saw as the tension on Summer's face fell into despondency. Tidus held his stare, and the other coven members revealed varied expressions of disapproval, disrespect, and... Malicious glee. Jensen found that worrying. She had an instinct to run, and she took a slight step backward in preparation.

"Seize her."

Bonding magic rose up from where she stood. She could feel the concerted effort of a dozen wills weave a web around her. She didn't know if other witches could 'see' magic the way she did, but terror gripped her as red tendrils formed a seal of entrapment around her. As the violent lines of those arcane symbols glowed brighter and a numbing pull dragged her limbs downward, forcing her to her knees, she rapidly lost the energy to resist. Paralysis set in and left her on the ground. Her vision became blurry, but she felt arms fold around her. She was being carried, but her lids did not stay open long enough to notice where she was being taken.

Only tingling sensations raced down her skin. She felt the slight brush of rough fingers and coarse material and then noticed as she was laid on velvet. Darkness descended as a lid closed on top of her, suffocating the light. The coven had placed her in a coffin.

Jensen lay motionless, unable to move, much less escape. She couldn't hear much but didn't fail to notice when the sonorous incantations started. She pinched her eyes shut, furiously trying to connect to her magic in an attempt to escape. Faced with the full force of her coven, she concluded that she might need to amplify her efforts. Pushing her consciousness outward, she prodded the key's dormant energies in her pocket and came up empty. Its presence was gone. Opening her mind, she could not even hear the faintest whispers from the spirit realm. Her powers had been limited, subdued, and bounded by the trap of the other Gate Guardians.

Pain flashed through her then, lancing through every cell and searing her nerve endings. She screamed but heard nothing but the silent whimper within that confined space. Outside, the incantations became louder, repetitive, and forceful. Her torso arched upward in her suffering. It felt like her blood was being drawn a hundred times over—a thousand. Then she understood. Her magic was being extracted. They were stripping her of her power. She wanted to pound on the coffin's lid and sides, but none of her movements were voluntary. She merely quaked and spasmed as the energies were drained from her. Whether it lasted minutes or even an hour, she was uncertain. The tortuous theft of her powers could have lasted an eternity by the likes of how it felt. At some point, it just finally ceased.

The lid opened, and Jensen was unsure if the brightness that greeted her had an ambiguous meaning. Was she dead? She felt like it. Or perhaps it was just the glaring fluorescent light of one of the funeral home's many rooms. Someone lifted her up, and her head merely lolled back lifelessly.

They passed through multiple doorways. More than Jensen remembered actually existed within the mortuary. There was an odd sensation of feeling like she was being taken down. She didn't remember there being multiple levels to the place. It was a single story with only a basement, but the descent never had so many stairs. When they finally reached level ground, a chill surrounded her. She was lowered down and felt the cold bite of a smooth stone floor. Footsteps retreated, and a door closed.

Jensen lay in the middle of that room that was alien to her, unsure where she had been locked up as consciousness left her.

9

DARK NIGHT OF THE SOUL

W hen Jensen awoke, it took her a moment to figure out where she had been taken. In some distant memory, she remembered thinking that it could possibly be the basement. As her eyes adjusted, the lack of light and the frigid air was the first clues that she had been terribly mistaken. A single bulb swayed to and fro from the ceiling. Though it only dimly illuminated her surroundings, she could deduce enough from her environment to know that she had been placed inside a dungeon.

With some effort, she sat upright. Even more, she managed to stand. As she took a step forward, an invisible barrier kicked her back. She fell, landing hard enough on the floor to have the wind knocked out of her. When she looked down, she saw the familiar bonding seal etched on the ground. The red runes flared up, glowing almost mockingly before they faded as the spell's retaliation diminished. She had been placed in the perfect prison—one that did not erect punishment with bars, but instead utilized psychological torment.

She felt hopeless. Casting her eyes to the ceiling, her gaze fixed on the dangling bulb swinging in the dark space above her. As she watched that pendulous motion, she began to wonder why the light would be swaying when there was no force to give it movement.

She found her answer as the light was unable to pierce a patch of darkness above. Gasping, she crawled backward. The dark shape detached from the ceiling and slithered down until she sensed it in front of the far wall across from her. Even in silence, there was sound, but even that disappeared as another presence manifested in the dungeon with her.

The wait was excruciating. Then she heard the slow thuds of heavy feet landing on the stone as something walked toward her. The darkness solidified and manifested as a tall figure emerging in front of her. All its features obscured save for horrible eyes that reflected in the dark. Even without her powers, she could never mistake the feeling of that presence. This time, she would not be able to defend herself against the demon. Some part of her hoped that the bonding enchantment did as well in keeping things out as keeping things in.

Whatever it was, it didn't speak or move. Jensen finally rasped, "What do you want, hell-spawn?"

"To see you suffer. I envy those who were lucky enough to cause it."

"The world is on the fringe of chaos, and you chose to come here to watch me squirm in the dark? I find that...pathetic." She wasn't sure how wise it was to insult a demon when she didn't have the upper hand. But she didn't see herself having much more to lose at this point. Her powers were taken, along with the Reaper's Key. She realized the artifact was missing as her hand pressed against pocketed air in the empty space that used to hold the key.

The demon chuckled. "The things you find and the things you think—none of it really matters, it would appear. Your coven listened only to the facts that confirm their suspicions, or else give them cause to act according to their bias. You are just a powerless little witch once more, the last Gate Guardian stripped of her legacy. You are a failure."

"Your manipulations won't work."

"They don't need to. Your kind does a beautiful job of manipulating themselves. Threatened with knowledge of impending doom, your own people have taken everything from you. You tricked yourself into believing that they will unravel the plans that have been set in motion."

"So you have come here like some sadistic glutton? Were you hoping to satiate your appetite for suffering through my misfortune?"

"Sweet girl... I have come to *thank* you. Without your rash and foolhardy action, I would not have been able to claim this world in all its soon-to-be apocalyptic splendor."

Jensen averted her gaze, folding in on herself to block out the demon's taunts. "Just leave, please."

The demon swooped close, and she could feel its vile breath creeping across her skin as it hovered close, finding glee in her misery. "Your decision to leave the gates open was questionable. So many souls would have escaped my grasp and slipped through to the other side to be claimed by those worthless beasts in the nether realm. But now...you no longer have the ability to stop it. The gates shall close and trap the hapless souls of the departed on this plane. Now that I roam here through my dark covenant with that bitch that has made your people her nemesis, I will claim each one of them!"

"They will stop you," Jensen countered feebly. "My powers are not gone. They reside in the hands of another. They will use it against you. They will prevent you from making the earth your playground."

"Fool! Your coven has convinced you of their purpose to protect the dead, but hear me now when I tell you that I shall make them my shepherds. They will hoard the dead on this plane, subdue them in their anguish. As the misery and insanity of those unfortunate souls echo and haunt the earth, I will be their savior. I will offer them the sweet release of their confinement by dragging them into the ravenous pits of hell!" The demon's smooth and venomous voice had become a roar.

Jensen struggled to speak as she was forced down by the demon's psychic force but continued her challenge. "The Gravetide spell...will call forth things far worse than you... You will fight for dominion over the spirits that will come here. The spirits are stuck in limbo...they will not be brought to heel so easily."

An evil laugh erupted from the demon and resonated in hollow echoes around that dark pit. "Naive little witch. The only thing that protects your kind from damnation is your mortal flesh and its divine ties to the realm of spirits. Without their vessels, their powers will evaporate like mist in front of hellfire. Their passage through the veil is all that kept them from falling into our clutches. When the spell recalls them, we shall claim those that have evaded usss," it hissed.

Despite her fear, Jensen pushed back, trying to break through the demon's psychic hold. "There will... *always*... be someone to stop you!"

"Let them come! I will have what is *mine!*" The demon

leaned in to bring its snarling mouth right next to her ear. As its hot and putrid breath brushed over her face, it stroked a long, tapering finger through her hair as it left her its final whisper. "When all has descended into chaos, I will come for you...I will slash through your frail little skin and rip out the last slivers of your soul to consume *myself!*"

Its presence retreated and left a hot whirlwind in its wake that settled down and left her shaken. The light above swayed violently, causing her shadow to dance wildly on the floor. A sweat had broken out over her forehead, and she felt her blouse cling to her drenched back. She thought it was over until a banging echoed from the door at the top of the staircase.

She jumped at the sudden noise. She had hoped for a brief moment, only a slight reprieve, but they had come again. She didn't know what they could still take from her. All was lost, and she could only foresee pandemonium on the surface if she could ever manage to escape. The furious pounding continued until a door shattered, and a metal bolt clanged over the steps. Light flooded in from the top, even though it could not penetrate all the shadows in the deep bowels of her prison.

A figure charged down, his feet flying over the steps before he suddenly stopped and looked over. "Jensen! Oh, my God. What the hell have they done?" He closed the gap between them. She wanted to warn him about the barrier, but he was at her side without anything blocking him. Putting a hand at her back, Emerson nudged her gently to sit upright. His golden hair hung in a tangled mess on his face, with some clinging to the sweat on his forehead. She could see that he had exerted himself to bash through the door above.

"After I told them of all I knew, and the decision I made, they turned on me," she said.

"*Who?* Your coven?"

"Yes."

"Dammit. Fuck them!" Jensen couldn't remember Emerson ever being so angry. "Here, let me help you up. We need to get out of here, in case they come back."

"Emerson, I won't be able to get out. They've placed an enchantment around me. I'm trapped."

His brow furrowed. "But there is no magic here. I don't sense anything. Jensen, I don't understand. Can't you feel the absence of magic?"

It was Jensen's turn to look confused. She moved forward and found no resistance. The barrier spell had been lifted. "It must have been the demon... His psyche must have ripped through the fabric of the spell."

"The...*what?*" His eyes went wide.

"It came back," she said solemnly. "It came to taunt me."

"Didn't you have to drive it back again? It didn't attack you like before?"

"It didn't need to. I don't pose a threat anymore without my powers."

"No! Those bastards stole it..."

"Yes, and they took the key. They want to shut the gate —indefinitely."

His hands flew to his head in dismay. "Jesus! I just can't —" He managed to compose himself after mumbling a few curses. "Ok. Look. Let's get out of here first."

"Please."

As they ran up, she saw the aftermath of Emerson's rescue. The heavy wooden door was shattered, with its metal fixings completely bent. "Emerson, how the hell did you..."

"Let's get out of here first." Running through, she realized they were in a cordoned-off section of the mortuary. She didn't recognize their surroundings until they charged through another door that brought them to Summer's office. A glance back revealed a secret entrance, with the wall rug ripped from the wall to reveal the door. Jensen found it amazing that she didn't know about any of this since working in the place nearly every day. The mortuary was abandoned entirely.

She expected to find someone, something, anything guarding the place—but the funeral home was empty. She knew the ley lines that ran through the place and that Emerson must have been sensed as he bulldozed through. Yet, no defenses met them, and they charged unperturbed towards Emerson's car through the front door.

Emerson rammed his foot into the accelerator as soon as the car sprang to life. They had turned around three corners before she finally posed him a question. Something had bugged her about what he had said, but moments before, "Emerson, how did you know the spell was broken—the bonding enchantment?"

"Well, the same way that I know how to get your powers back."

She was flabbergasted. She merely looked at him with a stunned expression on her face before he finally broke the suspense. "Listen, Jensen, all is *not* lost. But the decision lies with you. Magic can never truly be taken from a person. They might have siphoned a lot of it, but it can be replenished. Your coven may have thought they solved the problem by placing your powers in another. Still, the transference of your abilities as a Gate Guardian will only ever be temporary. If anyone made a mistake here today, it is them."

For once, Jensen wasn't sure how to respond. She merely

looked at him a moment longer before nodding and looking out through the windshield as they were driving. After a moment, she simply commented, "I think two legacies have just come into their power of late."

He nodded, knowing who she was referring to. "Yeah. Everything changes now."

10

DEATH'S GAMBIT

Once again, Emerson Allen revealed but one of his many secrets. This time, it manifested in a storage space on the outskirts of town. The unknown road they took wound right into the forest and eventually brought them to a small log cabin surrounded by the dense cluster of trees and foliage. Whoever lived there clearly wanted to avoid prying eyes. She half-expected them to go in, but instead, Emerson took them around the house and onto a footpath that led deeper in among the trees. An even smaller cabin greeted their eyes, appearing even older than the cabin. He managed to get them in after meddling with the lock, and despite the number of surprises that the last few days had in store, a few still seemed reserved for this moment.

They looked as though they had walked into a store of occult antiquities. Various paraphernalia and miscellaneous objects were stacked on the shelves and pushed into corners. Bottles and jars, all unlabeled, lined installed cupboards that had no doors. Volume upon volume of books and journals were all piled in ragtag niches on the floor. Everything was covered in a decent layer of dust, except the ritual circle inlaid in the middle of the cottage. Oddly enough, there wasn't a speck of grime or dust on that part of the floor. Jensen was sure her witch senses would have fired off among all that magic.

"How long have you been keeping all this a secret?"

"Well," he smirked, "to be honest, Mills, we've only known each other less than a week. Besides, a shit ton of stuff happened in the last few days alone. It didn't exactly pop into my mind to tell you about this place. At least, not until now."

She acknowledged that much. He had a point. As much as they had been through in a witch's trial by fire, they did not really have a chance to work in one of those drunk nights where friends divulge their deepest secrets to one another. "I'm going to take a wild guess... Your father?"

He nodded. "This was his place, and before him, it belonged to my grandfather. But everything in here spans back generations. I only discovered it a year ago. To be honest, I hadn't come here since, not even to look whether anything inside here was taken. I haven't been drawn back here until now."

"Emerson, back in the mortuary. You've never been inside that place. You didn't know how to navigate the corridors, much less what each room was used for. Yet somehow, you charged in, you knew how to find a door hidden behind a tapestry, and you knew that it led to a passageway that, in turn, would take you to a dungeon. The door was made of solid wood panels—thick beams held together by metal framing and inlays. You shattered the entire thing. *Shattered.* By pounding your shoulder against it to break through? Leaving only large splinters and metal beams behind?"

"Um, well, I wasn't exactly going to bash my shoulder

against it to get through. So I used an incantation to obliterate it."

Jensen just stared at him, slack-jawed, before answering. "That's all? That's your reaction? Emerson, you *cast*... Don't you feel a certain kind of way about that?"

"It's all very new," he admitted. "That's how I found you, by the way. I sensed something was wrong a few hours after you left. As time went by, this feeling started to grow that presaged something terrible, leaving a vivid impression of you on my mind. I didn't think much of it as I followed its calling. It led me to the mortuary. Your coven was obviously gone by the time I arrived. Going in, it was like following a trail of breadcrumbs that had been pecked at savagely by a flock of birds—like your magical trace had been damaged. I found the tapestry and ripped it off without thinking. I almost ran down that secret corridor as I sensed you were close, and then I hit that door. I—I pounded at it for minutes on end, not knowing how to get in. Standing next to it, I could feel a wrongness in the air, just on the other side. I only pushed and pounded harder." He was talking about the demon. She shuddered, knowing that the manifestation of that evil was so potent that she didn't even notice the sounds of his attempted rescue. "When I finally leaned against that door, exhausted, I started realizing that something was different about me."

He looked at his hands then, and she heard her own sharp intake of breath as she saw the scorch marks that ravaged his skin. "I think... I just opened myself to whatever was stirring inside. My lips moved by themselves, and somehow I mouthed the spell that summoned the force to break that door open."

Jensen pushed her hair back then and considered him

with amazement. "Emerson, did you know you were a mage?"

"I had suspicions. Like I told you, I know I descended from a special line of witches—potentially those well versed in battle magic—but I was never sure."

"Maybe that is why Elsie wanted you to leave when we found ourselves in the alley, and perhaps why Tidus insisted on keeping you detained from getting involved in Gate Guardian business. I think—even as a legacy—you posed a serious threat."

He blushed, looking slightly uncomfortable with the attention. "Um, well, anyway. I think we may be able to help you here. Especially with this." He pointed to the arcane sigil in the middle of the floor.

"Don't you find it strange that it is the only thing in this room that doesn't have a speck of dust on the floor? It's like something has moved here quite recently."

"You're not wrong. However, it is not anything physical. Remember when you told me how there were magical traces left at the cemetery—where the desecrated graves formed the tainted pentacle?"

"Yes."

"Well, imagine that happening here, with magic intensified a hundredfold. The traces you saw in the graveyard were fading. Because this sigil is carved in the very woodwork, it retains the spells' residual magic near it. The potency of that stored power dwells here as if it is alive."

"It's...almost like the Reaper's Key. This is some kind of relic."

Emerson nodded. "Of a sort. The relic is not tied to this place and the floorboards, however. According to my father's journal, it is only the sigil itself that is powerful. If I should draw a line here, for instance,"—he pointed at the mark to illustrate —" or break it, then all the magic would be released at once and flow back into the ether. Right now, it is a fully charged battery. A conduit. We're going to use it to jumpstart your magic."

Jensen sighed heavily. "Emerson, it's the sixth day." She had noticed that the sun had only just risen as they had left the mortuary. "We've nearly run out of time. If I do get my powers back, I wouldn't even know what to do with it. The Key is gone. So is any form of help. The coven was our last resort. And I don't even know what happened to Friar Ambrose. After reading his letter yesterday, I got the faintest idea that something was after him as well."

"I couldn't get a hold of him. I tried right after we split up. But we cannot give up, Jensen. We're already facing a hopeless case. It cannot get worse than it already is, so we have to fight to try to make it better." He walked over to one of the shelves, and from it, he removed the largest tome in the room. As he let it fall on a close by table, he swooped his hands over the pages. They fluttered rapidly until they opened on a picture of the sigil. Within, there was a diagram. It illustrated a single witch standing in the middle, receiving the energies that were stored.

"It's a transference spell?" Jensen acknowledged with uncertainty.

"Not a spell exactly. More of a meditative ritual. This seal is a magical vault. They are really rare as it is. This one has been soaking up the energies from spells for decades now— perhaps even a century. Anyway, because they are rare, a spell has never been written for one. Odd enough. Instead, a witch needs to prove their worth by connecting to the deepest traces of magic within them. In a way, this is going to be a test." Emerson looked at her seriously then. "If you want your powers back, you are going to have to prove that you really need it."

Jensen was never one to feel afraid without cause. Confronted with this, however, she felt apprehensive for the first time. The truth was that a part of her didn't want to connect with whatever latent energies were left attached to her spirit. The burden of the task ahead was daunting, and the decision carried a weight that was too significant for her to wrap her mind around. In her heart of hearts, she didn't know how to prove that she wanted to re-invoke her powers. Yet, she had no choice. Her coven's actions bordered on the insane and the desperate. Hell was dangerously close to rising uninvited, and magic-crazed witches were running rampant to fulfill delusional pipedreams.

"Let's just do it," she said.

He smiled. "Good, we just need—"

"To hurry. We are running out of time. Listen, I need to do this now. I need to throw my entire supply of willpower behind this; otherwise, I may tap out."

"Mills, this circle of power is dangerous. We need to be ready. Let's just make sure we understand all—"

"Listen, Emerson. I'm impatient. I'm rash. I make passionate choices on a whim because I am surrounded by people who wait too long before acting. That is what my coven did and look at where their actions got us. Two novices had to throw everything at finding out what lies in store, and we have only just come into ourselves. Quite frankly, I don't think we've been doing badly either. Let me do this—without deliberation or doubts. You say we need to be ready? People have waited for eons to be ready without action, and that never brought them any closer to resolution."

Perhaps there was still a part of Emerson that wanted to

argue, but she could see as he fought with himself to see the reason in her words. "Let's get started then," he said. "Step into the middle of the circle." He picked up the book and traced his finger over the inscriptions within the margins and bottom. He looked around and produced a thick glass vial filled with red liquid. "This is a hallucinogenic agent. Because your magic is completely dormant, we need to put you in an altered state that will form a stronger connection to your spirit. Where your magic will be rooted. Once you slip into that state, I need you to focus. You will need to reignite the flame of your magic. Right now, it's but an ember that glows dimly in your spirit. I need you to fan it until it sparks again."

Jensen took the bottle. "Seems simple enough."

Emerson raised an eyebrow at her. "Have you ever taken hallucinogens before? Like 'shrooms?"

"Nope."

He chuckled in a way that conveyed that he knew something she didn't. "Look, when you drink this, everything becomes more vibrant. What's left of your magic will seem like a candle flame flickering among neon lights in a club."

Taking a deep breath, she popped off the stopper and threw the concoction down the back of her throat. "Alright then, here we go."

Emerson was speechless. His jaw hung slack as he merely looked at her and took the empty vial she handed back to him. The entire image changed in an instant. He glowed, and then it appeared as though he was set aflame. For a moment, Jensen panicked, until he started talking. "It's already kicking in. Dammit, Jensen." His magical aura swirled around him in a blazing firestorm, and parts of it seemed to meld and swirl into his surroundings. Around her, the world pulsed with color, or perhaps that was her own pulse increasing.

"Jensen, Jensen! Over here, look at me. Focus. Adjust. Forget what you think you see and remember where you are."

She felt like she was in the middle of a kaleidoscope. Every turn of her head made the world shift into a different iridescent pattern. Emerson was watching her every move. She could feel his gentle grip on her shoulders, and she stared into his bright face that was aglow with what she was starting to think was magic. *Magic.* That was what she was looking at. The energy that coursed through him was blazing on his features. With her untrained eye, she was unable to filter and structure her vision around it.

He still held her, making sure she wouldn't tip over. "You're doing alright. Close your eyes now. I need you to concentrate. Take everything you're feeling and direct it inward, despite how confusing they may seem."

She followed his instruction. Even though she managed to shut out the vision of the spectrum that raged around her, the darkness behind her lids held tiny sparks that flew around in a firework display. She knew she needed to calm her mind. She focused on her heartbeat, ticking steadily like a metronome. Allowing the erratic reactions of her senses to fall in line with that sound, she followed the impression inward to where it thumped in her chest. For the moment, all else melted away, with only the awareness of her physical vessel remaining.

At first, there was nothing, nothing but disconnected sensations that drifted to her from outer experiences. Meanwhile, her awareness was lost within. She began to worry that she would be stuck in the limbo of her own mind. That was until she noticed a warmth rising from her base. She latched onto it, thinking that it was the stored energies contained in the seal. Following, she found it—a small and insignificant glimmer in the darkness. It sensed her, that single particle of light flashing in recognition. Either it was growing, or she was moving closer. They were drawn to one another. Making contact, she absorbed the light. Her chest felt as if a furnace had just roared to life.

Her eyes flew open, and the once-dizzying display of color coalesced into the unmistakable interior of the cottage. Around her, the seal lines appeared to be vibrating and emitting heat as the magic from it was poured forth to replenish her. All at once, it stopped. She thought it was over until she saw herself fall onto the floor. She had fainted. Emerson dove forward and cradled her. His mouth opened wide as he voiced a shout to snap her out of her coma, but Jensen couldn't hear him. His words were all muted. Confusion gripped her until it dawned on her what was happening. She was having an out-of-body experience.

"Jensen."

She froze. It was a voice she could not mistake for anyone else. One she had heard once, only recently, after many years. She turned around. The willowy woman was excruciatingly beautiful. She had gray eyes, framed by rich brown locks that fell past her shoulders. There was a grace to her features that was unforgettable, even strangely intimidating. She immediately left you with the impression that she had a strong inner fire—one which could oscillate between a caring warmth or a fervent retaliation against oppression. Jensen had inherited virtually nothing from her mother, except for the latter. Perhaps it was the kindred connection of their mutually shared zeal that now brought her here to look upon her daughter after so many years.

"Mom."

The woman looked at Jensen's unconscious body. "You've been through quite the ordeal, honey."

The address of endearment felt odd, its affection strange. Still, this was her mother. "You have no idea. I... don't really know what to say."

"Maybe there is something you'd like to ask instead."

Of course, there is, Jensen thought. Yet, she didn't really have the luxury of time on her side. Seeing her mother in front of her, not merely as a memory or apparition, a thousand emotion-laden questions formed in her mind.

"This won't be the last time we'll see each other," her mother added, smiling as if reading her mind. Jensen knew that she had heard what she needed to, so instead, she asked the most practical thing relevant to the present moment. "How do I get back in?"

"You have to be ready."

She felt irritated hearing that. "Ready? Have I not proven that? I absorbed the magic from the circle. My powers were reawakened."

"I know, honey," her mom responded, showing an understanding of the rising emotion Jensen could not make out herself. "Even when we have the power, we may not feel ready to use it."

Jensen was angry—not because she felt insulted, but because her mother was right. "The odds are stacked against us, Mom. I have no choice. I need to be ready *right now*."

Her mother stepped closer and placed a hand against her cheek. "When the time comes, you will be. But right now, I sense you are unsure."

"Of course, I am! A pretender is out there, imbued with my powers. I'm afraid that I won't be able to hold open the gate when someone pushes harder."

"Then become the gate."

"What?"

"Bond your essence with it, and determine who may open or close it. Make the gate as immovable as you are. You are the last Guardian of the Gate. Thus, the last decision always rests with you—despite the false belief of those who take power, they do not understand."

"You make it seem so simple by seeming so sure."

"I was unsure once, and I wish I hadn't been. You doubt what you need to do next. It is the only reason why your spirit won't settle back inside its vessel."

Jensen looked down at herself, chewing over her mother's words. Something finally clicked in place then. "This is what happened to you, isn't it? You couldn't go back. It wasn't just a coma."

Her mother offered a sad smile. "Let's make sure it doesn't happen to you."

In the next second, Jensen found herself staring into Emerson's eyes.

Everything assumed an entirely different tempo upon her awakening. The spirit world had been amplified to a stereo wail that was near-deafening. Jensen immediately knew that the dead were being manipulated. It wasn't long before she and Emerson jumped into his car to drive back into Bayside. Tuning into the protests from the spirits, she managed to navigate them through the streets. Since reconnecting with her guardian magic, her powers had been a way pointer. It brought them to the inner belly of the city with not a minute to spare. The streets were brimming with the souls of the dead.

Emerson slammed on the brakes. "God, I nearly drove into that guy!"

"He's a spirit, Emerson. Death is kind of a good insurance plan to cover accidents. He'll walk it off." The spirit in question wandered off, blissfully unaware of the car that had stopped mere inches from him. He melded with the horde that waded through the street.

"Did your mom happen to mention anything about this?" Emerson asked, his knuckles white as he gripped the steering wheel.

"No. I guess it's up to you and me, Detective. Listen, I don't know how comfortable you've become in your own abilities in the last few hours, but I can certainly use a mage right now."

"I'm still a wild card with a spell. Do you think it's a bright idea for me to be attacking spirits?"

"It's not the spirits I'm concerned about. I can handle the dead. Who do you think has been calling them forth?" The question was entirely rhetorical; they both knew the answer as more souls were pouring forth from the necromancer alley.

"You have your powers back," he acknowledged, "so how do you plan on using it to deal with them?"

"I've held onto the Reaper's Key long enough to learn a few tricks," she answered. Her door was already ajar, and she was ready to jump out when a violent spirit approached from the side. An invisible force pushed it back before she even had time to react. It was phased for only a second before attacking again. This time she was ready. She responded by using its anger to propel it right through the veil, feeling as its momentum carried it through to the other side. She whipped around and caught Emerson with his hands raised.

"Looks like I'm not the only one with a trick up my sleeve."

Emerson's eyes were wide. "I'm not used to 'seeing' them. Was this what it was like in the alley?" There was an almost comical tremble to his voice. She had to force back a grin. Death magic wasn't for every witch.

"I hate to break it to you, but this is a whole lot worse. These fanatics have started to empty limbo. We need to stop them."

Neither of them felt like climbing out of the car as they looked out across the sea of souls. After banishing the attacking spirit, they had attracted attention to themselves. The others were glaring at them.

Emerson gulped. If he was afraid, he was trying hard not to show it. Jensen didn't blame him. She was reasonably sure she was trying to save face as well. The spirits were threatening—not because of the suddenness by which they attacked, but in the moments of absolute and unnatural stillness that preceded it—when they were just watching. It was unnerving.

"Emerson, we're walking into untamed territory here. I need you to be the ringmaster," Jensen said. They were different from the spirits she had encountered in the spirit realm. A melancholy tied itself to them that made no secret about their dislike of being back on this plane. However, with the tension eased as if by some unseen command, they continued to wander around.

Emerson nodded. "I can't hurt or banish them, but I can try to push them back."

"That will be enough."

"How many can you send over at a time?"

"I'll have to pace it. If I do what I did in the alley, without a conduit, I'll exhaust myself. We're going to attract attention eventually, so I can't be left powerless. Neither can you. Let's diminish the numbers first, and then even the odds."

She crept closer tentatively until she came upon the first soul. Strengthening a connection with her magic, she reached out toward its incorporeal body. The spirit faded. Its crossing reminding her of a dying breath being blown out. It left her with a sense of pathos. It weighed heavily on her for a while before it dissipated too. "This is going to be harder than I thought." It was like severing the emotional ties that the soul had to this world, forcing them to let go of their unresolved emotion.

She presented herself to each, acting as the bridge by which they could cross back into the spirit realm. Some noticed, sane enough to recognize an avenue of release and approaching her freely. Others were already crazed by their time here, or subjected too strongly to the influence of their earthly slavers, and moved closer with harmful intent. Emerson managed to block them long enough until Jensen could weed them out one by one. The spirits charged with stronger emotions dissipated in a ghostly fog that drifted to the sky. The air above had come alive like an aurora, framing the blood moon that now peaked from the clouds. It was a spectacle that soon drew the necromancers from their alley as an alarm was raised.

"Here they come!" Emerson shouted.

Jensen looked toward the alley, and sure enough, a dozen or more were charging forward. It was less than she expected. She had a suspicion the rest were already involved in the progress of the blood spell. Instead of attacking, the group lined up opposite them and started chanting. The spirits reacted, and as one, they turned on both of them.

Emerson came up behind her. "Uh-oh."

Wicked looks lined the faces of the chanting necromancers. In turn, the spirits' expressionless faces were blank slates upon which their masters' intentions could be written. In the silent minute that followed, not much was left to the imagination regarding what the necromancers were instructing the spirits to do. It was all Jensen and Emerson could muster to keep them back once they barreled forward.

They ran in the opposite direction, trying to put distance between them and the souls. Neither of them knew how to outrun the dead, but they certainly tried. As Jensen looked desperately around her for an alternative plan, it was Emerson that dragged them to a halt. She flew around, regarding him with desperate confusion.

"Use me. As the conduit."

"*What*?"

"There is no time to discuss this." He took her hand. "Here. Use my power to manifest your ability. I'll draw on yours to use mine." He gave a solemn smile. He was crazy, stupidly brave, and impulsively clever. She turned just as the souls were about to wash over them.

She felt her own spirit being pulled taut as Emerson drew on her power to erect a shield. This time, the spiritual force could not drive the throng of spirits back, but it kept the two witches from being overwhelmed. At once, Jensen understood what Emerson had meant. Focusing, she tapped into his magic to magnify her own. She reached her hand out to where the force field connected to the assaulting energies from the dead and willed them through the veil. The apparitions dispersed like so much smoke, their energies swirling back into limbo. Hundreds more stood in front of them and filled the gap left by the front line. United in their effort, the two witches renewed their counteroffensive. The magical force that Emerson created acted as a conductor for her own magic and broadened its effects.

Melding their powers, they drove back throngs of the departed until the streets started to empty of their cold presence.

The necromancers looked on in horror as they tried to force their will on the remaining dead, pressing them harder. Emerson and Jensen advanced, step by step, pushing them back and guiding them to the other side. As the army of souls thinned, the witches who spoke to manipulate them stood hesitantly until they started to retreat.

"They're falling back!" Jensen shouted.

"This isn't over yet! The moon is out, and they must have started the spell. We need to stop it! More dead are flowing through the gates."

"I can sense it. You're right."

Then the impossible happened. It was as though a translucent sheath was pulled over the sky, and the moon appeared to be a glowing ember that was about to burn through black fabric. The street lights seemed to flicker, sputter, and then dim completely. Heaviness clung to the air, then settled down, forcing a pressure on them that was difficult to resist. It muffled the sound, and then caused their ears to ring as they felt something approach. Jensen looked toward the necromancers, seeing as the few remaining stragglers succumbed to the effects of the unseen force as well.

"W—what the hell is that? The Gravetide spell?" Emerson asked.

"No. I would have felt the veil drop. Something worse is on its way... and it's stronger than ever before."

Even the spirits reacted. Without the necromancers' incantation, they weren't the hapless victims of their manipulation any longer. Whatever was approaching had driven them to their knees, and they were holding their heads between their hands as if to block out the torment. She believed they had regained their will, only for it to be subjected to another torture.

Something caught Jensen's eye down the street. At first, it was a shapeless object that seemed to shift in the wind until Jensen identified it as a billowing black cloak. It was attached to the shoulders of a figure that glided with a threatening intent. As the obscurity was drawn from its features, Jensen could make out the unmistakable scowl and contempt that permanently fixed itself on the face of Elsie Turner. In that wavering light, with wild hair and vengeance in her eyes, she looked every bit like a dark goddess.

It was nothing compared to the force that crept behind her. A wall of black smoke rolled ominously in her wake, enveloping the souls that didn't cross. As it consumed them, one by one, flashes of energy illuminated the dark smog within. Something dwelled inside a long shadow, with every flash revealing another horrible detail to its figure. It was immediately daunting as it was unmistakably familiar. Jensen watched the demon trailing behind Elsie, and then she felt its anger spewing forth as it touched her mind.

This is not over yet, she thought. Not over my dead body.

11

THE LAST GUARDIAN

"Did I not warn you not to meddle in our affairs?" Elsie asked, cocking her head to the side, her look venomous.

"Did you not realize that I wouldn't be able to keep myself from meddling?" Jensen countered.

"Your hubris will be your undoing. The spell is already in motion. You cannot halt the inevitable. The gate is ours!"

"That's strange, 'cause the army that you called forth seems to be disappearing." Emerson stepped forward, standing shoulder to shoulder with Jensen to face the old necromancer.

Elsie regarded him with amused incredulity. "You think we have come to rely on a handful of ghosts at our bidding? Ha! An army is only needed by the fool who has to claw his way to power. I already have the upper hand, boy."

"You mean the lackey that skulks at your back?" Jensen challenged. "Your little 'pet' may have given you a false idea of victory."

Red lightning flashed amid the black smoke to reveal the demon's fearsome form, almost conveying its hostility at her brazenness. However, it didn't speak. Jensen thought it odd. She suspected that the demon was still maintaining its duplicitous guise, despite Elsie's egocentric perception of control.

Elsie smiled with malicious content. Clearly, she knew something Jensen didn't. "Let me show you what offers me my ideas of victory." With those words, the street lights surrounding the witch flickered in an epileptic pulse. To Jensen's dismay, it briefly illuminated the faces on the edges of the smog that she found familiar. They churned and pushed against the smoky barrier, surrounded by its dark confines. At first, she discounted these as the random souls of other witches until she saw Tidus's face. Those of other members followed: The witches who had seized and siphoned her power, and Desmond and Lenora. Her coven was under the sway of the demon's control.

"*No...*" Reaching out, she expected to hear a resounding call for help. But the spirits of her coven were violent. They lashed out against her, meeting her help with vehemence and conveyance of intense loathing. She retracted her consciousness, taken aback by their enmity and anger.

"Do you see now the futility of your efforts? Even your coven has turned on you. They have seen the glorious yields of our purpose."

"Fucking turncoats," Emerson said, gritting his teeth.

But to what end? Jensen thought. *Why would they do this? Do they know the aversion the necromancers feel toward the Gate Guardians?* As the thought crossed her mind, a crowd of necromancers spilled forth from the alley. They stopped in their tracks as they saw Elsie and the thick black mass of the demonic presence. From their reaction, it was clear to her that whatever was unfolding did not harbor their knowledge. At the front stood Alison, equally perplexed by what she was seeing. Her eyes met Jensen's then, and perhaps it was the first time that it was filled with a desperation to understand instead of the usual mischief and hostility.

At that moment, the dark mass swirled, and from the vortex stepped forth a young man.

"Who is that?" Emerson asked tensely.

Jensen knew but couldn't bring herself to voice the answer. Her mind was ravaged by the deep betrayal that now seemed solidified as Armand's pale face emerged from the darkness.

"I see you recognize our new acolyte," Elsie teased.

"I thought he was dead."

"I told you, Mills, that I can face the challenges that beset me—even Death. Once more, you also seem to have little to offer. I will do what you could not."

He had been imbued with her powers. There was enough in his words that hinted at that. Beyond that fact, she could sense the shape of her magic flowing through him —even though it seemed...mangled. "The sacrifice. You gave your life, so you may become the key to closing the gate." His death was a ruse. The Gate Guardians had taken his corpse, only to raise it when her powers manifested. No one needed to spell out the truth. Somehow, the unfolding events just seemed to fall in place.

"My spirit has returned to my vessel, imbued with the secrets of the nether," Armand said. "With it, I shall become the new master of the dead!"

His soul belongs to usss! The sudden hiss of a voice startled her until she tied its sinister cadence to the demon. *With it, we shall seal the gate, and the bounty of the earth will be mine alone!* His announcement was unexpected, and she waited for a reaction from the demon's depraved minions.

But it was like they couldn't hear him. She then realized that his voice had echoed in her mind alone.

"Witness now," Elsie began, "as the twilight of the Gate Guardians has arrived. A new order of witches shall rise, and the ancestral dead shall be their gods!"

"Jensen!" Emerson whispered. "Did you hear the demon?"

"Yes. *Wait*. You did, too?" She was stunned.

He nodded. "I think the counter spells we launched linked our psyches. Their goals, they're—"

"—completely misaligned," she said in a hushed tone, completing his thought. "They all think they're winning, each giving stock to their own story. Every one of them believes they are the main victors, but the only outcome of this is hell on earth."

"I see the hour is nigh..." Elsie's eyes gleamed in anticipation.

"Uh...Mills..." Emerson stammered. Jensen looked at him before following his gaze that was directed to their backs. Behind them, the entire street was lined with the dead. Thousands of lifeless eyes stared at them, awaiting a command from their jailers. Distracted by the arrival of Elsie and her demon, the necromancers must have emptied limbo. They were on the threshold of chaos. The realization had barely dawned before the very sky shattered, and Jensen felt the veil starting to rip. The moon assumed a bloodthirsty glow and threatened to scorch the sky around it.

"Children!" Elsie shouted, addressing the necromancers. "Make an example of the empty courage of these fools. Let the last Gate Guardian bow to you, and end the line of the Guardians once and for all!" The black cloud billowed as a roar emanated from its depths, announcing the demon's relish in their imminent triumph.

Not a single necromancer moved. The horde of screaming souls never descended. Emerson exhaled the breath he was holding, though he still stood ready to defend himself to the end. The necromancers didn't even look their way. They stared at Elsie, surrounded by the evil presence they sensed behind her. She leered at them in return, and even Armand's diabolical glee was twisted back into a baleful look. "What is the meaning of this? Attack, you worthless scum!"

Someone did react then. It was Alison. Determinedly, she stepped forward and made her way across the street—to where Jensen and Emerson stood. Face to face, the two women exchanged a long look layered with more meaning than either could decipher at that point. She reached inside her pocket and afterward held her hand out to Emerson, displaying the Reaper's Key resting on her palm. In that proximity, the runes to its sides started to glow as Jensen's magic intertwined with it once more. Alison nudged her to take the artifact, so she did. Resting in her hand, the powerful energies of the key seeped into her. She could at once sense the presence of the gates between the realms.

"What have you done? Fool!" Elsie howled, with eyes blazing at the younger member in her coven. Alison merely backed away and took her place among the gathered necromancers. Jensen gripped the key in her hand.

Madness ensued. Elsie uttered a rallying cry that shattered the windows of most cars and buildings parked in the street. As a shiver traveled down her spine, Jensen knew that it was a manifestation of Death Magic that she only ever read about once—the banshee scream. The necromancers' hands flew up to stopper their bleeding ears, sagging to the ground in agony at the unnatural sound. Next to her, even Emerson crumpled to the ground in agony. Jensen stood unperturbed as the dead charged forward, enraged to become wraiths that looked ready to tear them apart.

Her mouth shaped ancient words as she spoke to the key, and a spectral glow enveloped the artifact as the first spirit reached her. The assault broke at her feet. The violent energies of the spirits imploded and were then siphoned through the key. She could feel them crossing back into the other side, and above, the cracked dome of the sky seemed to mend as limbo was fed with its stolen spiritual energy.

Incapable of allowing the insult, the demon rolled forward to Elsie's dismay. A humongous black tentacle shot out from that dark blot. It coalesced into the large and emaciated horror that was the demon's physical form. It lunged at Armand and took the young witch's jaw between its clutches, forcing it open. All bore witness to the impossible horror of the demon climbing into the false guardian's mouth. By sacrificing himself, he had sold his soul to hell. The vessel became the demon's to claim. The dark smog followed, seeping into that figure that seemed so tiny in comparison to the force taking hold of him.

The witch reeled back, and then folded forward. All watched and waited. Armand soon raised his head, his face covered in a web of dark veins that signified his possession. The smile that broke out over that voice was so inhuman, so chilling, that the once boastful Elsie now took a step backward. Every Gate Guardian stood exposed in the vast emptiness left by the demonic presence. It now spoke with the mouth of another. "I will claim what is mine yet," it rumbled.

The demon's power surged into the ether and bashed against the gate to the other side that Jensen held open with her will. In her mind's eye, she could see as he was forcing it to shut, trying to toss the world into damnation while the blood moon was still at its apex. Jensen pushed back, drawing on all the might contained in the Reaper's Key. However, even with the help of the artifact, she could not hold on.

"Stupid little girl. The sacrifice has been made. It is the true key to herd the dead! There can be only one master of the gate! You give it NOTHING but your own weakness!"

As she strained against the demon's will, its jeering resounded in her mind. *A...sacrifice.* The words dawned on her like a revelation. *The true key...* She spared a glance at the artifact in her hand, shaped from the finger bones of one of her ancestors. *The only way to counter a blood spell is by blood. My blood,* she thought. But it couldn't be that simple. Drawing blood alone wouldn't undo the celestial force of the Gravetide spell. *Unless...the spell was already cast—*

"—When a key was fashioned," Emerson rasped, looking up at her. They were still mentally linked. He followed her entire self-deliberation. He tried his best at a smile. "But the key was never meant to be a thing."

"It was meant to be a person. A gate guardian." She regarded the key another second, then squeezed it hard until she felt the skin on her palm tear and see the blood flowing down her wrist. *Blood shall be fought with blood.*

Then, she redirected the shape of her spell. She released her hold on the gate. She could hear the demon's maniacal laugh as he bought her false surrender. While he was basking in his hollow victory, she began weaving her energy around the key. She braided its essence with her own and felt as the bony artifact in her hand quivered. The runic symbols dissipated from its sides like burning paper. The bone turned brittle and fell into a small heap of dust before blowing from her palm. She felt the pain on her right hand after that, and her other hand grabbed the wrist to steady it as it trembled. She watched as the runes, once engraved on the key, now burned through her flesh. The piercing pain was momentary before it faded, leaving the runes emblazoned on her skin. The Reaper's Key had been reforged, and she wielded it in her own hand.

The gate to limbo was inches from closing, the veil nearly ripped in half, and mere seconds separated the moment from all hell breaking loose. Then Jensen jammed the gate. With her palm still cut, she could feel the connection with the blood magic at work. With her soul merged to the Reaper's Key—now a part of her bodily vessel—her consciousness seized hold of it. It was as if the gate was testing her intentions, asking her what she longed to do. There was a momentary titanic struggle as the demon held fast. It tried to deride her, battering her with insults in its black tongue. With a thought, one with all her magic driven behind it, she flung open the gate. The street quaked as the dead were swallowed back into the spirit world, crossing over in mass. The sea of spectral energies flowed back into limbo. The sky flashed as the veil resealed, and blood dripped from the moon until its pearly light bathed the surrounding city in its ghostly pallor. In that glare, Armand's possessed body buckled, and a demonic scream escaped his throat as the death magic that reanimated his body ceased to be. The dark covenant was broken. The demon was banished. The street, now empty, felt like a ghost town.

12

GRAVETIDE

"How did you do it?" Emerson asked.

Jensen rolled her eyes while helping him up. "Really?" she groaned. "That's the first thing you're going to say?"

"Arghhhh!" Elsie rushed at them unawares, donning a ritual dagger she drew from her side, holding it aloft in her attack charge. The blade flashed as it descended but never struck flesh. It rebounded, knocking the weapon from her hand and throwing Elsie a distance from their feet.

Alert, Jensen's head whipped in Emerson's direction. His hands were aloft, the tips of his fingers tingling with a spell of deflection he hurtled her way to protect her. His lips were still moving rapidly as he closed off the incantation until he lowered his arms back to his sides. He rushed forward and picked up the dagger Elsie had dropped. She remained in a heap on the road, her body wracked with frustrated sobs.

Jensen edged closer to the defeated woman, now cautious of her volatility. She kneeled beside her and waited until Elsie raised her wild eyes to meet Jensen's own.

"*What?*" she spat. "Do you wish to mock me for my failure? I was close. *So* close!"

"Really?" Jensen challenged. "Are you that certain? You made a deal with a demon. He may have even been responsible for the massacre of your family. In your grief, he could find you susceptible to his promises. You sealed a covenant that would have subjected this world to his whims." Looking up, she saw the Gate Guardians moving closer to listen in on their exchange. They had lost as much, she suspected. They had abandoned their creeds, in the face of desperation of an empty purpose. The raising of the dead, the murder of Armand, and the woods' attack—possibly faked—it was all a part of their scheme. What their gains would be, she had yet to find out. She knew, though, that every culprit in this saga had played a game with the other. "The demon, he was manipulating all of you to achieve exactly what he wanted."

"Impossible! He was under my control. I had him on a leash!"

"Then it broke the moment you put it on him. You believed he would bring back your people—your omnipotent ancestors—and perhaps he would have, but it would only be to claim you all in the end. He wanted the gates closed to trap the dead. It would have become his reaping ground. A role he would have stolen"—she began looking at Tidus—"from the Gate Guardians, except he had different ideas as to where the departed belonged."

Mixed emotions played on the faces of the members of her coven. She could see their internal struggle as they tried to make peace with their choices this night. "We did what we thought was right," her former coven leader responded in a measured tone.

"And look where that got you." It was Alison. Flanked by

a handful of necromancers, she approached the party in the middle of the road. "You were never any different from us!"

"Your people have no right to approach us, you filth!" Desmond spat.

"Filth?" Alison asked incredulously. "You were the one to fraternize with the demon, not us! We were never aware of the infernal contracts stepped into. Whatever our purpose, we have never relied on hell to get done what we could do ourselves." She had a point, and it was sharp enough to prick the elder witch's inflated grandiosity. He was left speechless. She turned to Jensen then. "We probably owe you more than we can repay—"

"You don't. Your debt was settled the moment you handed me the key. I don't always agree with your methods, or that of your coven. Still, you aligned yourself after your misdirection. Your people possess great power. Whatever you do from here, just do so wisely."

Alison gave a curt nod. There was no taint in the last look that Jensen exchanged with the necromancer. Neither was there any love lost between their factions. What they did have, at that moment, was an understanding. It was enough. Alison turned around and, followed by her people, flowed back into the alley. They disappeared nearly as quickly as the spirits had in their crossing.

"What happens to *us* now?" asked a young witch who stood among the Gate Guardians.

"Remember your place," Tidus responded, clearly fighting the impulse to say something scathing.

"He'll only be able to do that when you remember yours, to be a model for his behavior," Jensen chided.

"Girl, you will remember that I am—"

"You are nothing of significance to me," Jensen interrupted before he could dare complete the thought. "From here on, I am no longer affiliated with your coven. I will uncover my magic on my own."

"You may have been able to circumvent this crisis without a spell, but you still need proper tutelage in the incantations to guide the rest of your power."

"Not all magic is governed by words, Tidus. It is through words that the meaning of magic is misconstrued. Our history has proven that much, with every lie that circulated on the use of our powers and those who were deemed to have twisted it. Some magic merely needs the guidance of genuine intention. My abilities and magic are expressive."

"That is how you closed the gate, isn't it? You revealed your intentions through your heart alone?" Emerson asked, intrigued.

She nodded, keeping eye contact with her former leader. "The events that unfolded tonight did nothing but meddle with an order that was already established. For a moment, it managed to upset that balance. Still, it was too powerful to be unraveled so easily for dark purposes. The Gravetide spell was cast centuries ago. It would only ever be cast once. The ultimate sacrifice was made, and the result was the birth of the first true gate guardian. We are the true watchers over the dead, keeping vigil of their safe passage. I stand here as its legacy, the last of its bloodline. The last of the Gravetide."

Emerson regarded her with awe. She was sure he wanted to say a thousand things in response, but he was struck speechless.

"A lonesome witch does not fare well in our world. Every caster needs a coven." There was an almost simmering threat under Lenora's words. Perhaps it was a portent.

"From my experience," Emerson rebutted, "covens cause more harm than renegade witches. I think that became clear tonight. You are the ones that need policing. Rest assured that I will keep a close watch."

Tidus retaliated. "Insolent boy! We—"

"*You* would do well to pay heed to the words of the mage. He is more than capable of bringing justice to any of your numbers that fall out of line." Jensen walked closer until her face was mere inches from the imposing Gate Guardian. "Take this lesson now, from an upstart and insolent youth, and allow us to be an example to you of what it truly means to be a Gate Guardian."

Tidus's jaw tensed as he bit back the tender pieces left of his pride. He stepped back, and then motioned to his people to fall in step as he left. The Gate Guardians retreated. As they walked, their bodies sank into the ground until their forms seeped away beneath the surface, spiriting away. She guessed that traveling six feet under was a reasonably inconspicuous way to get around when your plans were as covert as the watchers' had been.

There was no one left in the street, save for Elsie, Emerson, and herself. The ousted necromancer had calmed notably, even though her eyes were still feral. She had been cheated and left with nothing save for her soul, which she could be thankful for.

Emerson was the first to speak. "Listen, Mills. I know we won, but I don't think we can let *her* out of our sight. She instigated a pretty intense series of events. She may have been susceptible to the promises of power and retribution. However, she was still charismatic enough to bring a lot of what happened to fruition. Besides, I, for one, still have many questions."

The last thing the two of them suspected was Elsie's reaction to his last words, which was a knowing and discomforting smile. Jensen felt alert again as she tried to scrutinize the expression of the other woman. "This isn't over, is it?"

"That's the funny thing about Death. With witches, nothing really is over. Every event set in motion, and every action to curtail it, is merely...postponed, until centuries later. Your ancestors made a blood pact and sacrificed themselves to create an infallible line of guardians. Yet still, you were challenged and even nearly killed. Over, you asked? Perhaps it is, for now. You see, you haven't exactly solved all the pieces of this puzzle."

"What puzzle?" Emerson seethed.

"None that I believe you're unfamiliar with, Detective," she goaded. "Just one you have been slow to put together, to become aware of the missing pieces."

"Don't listen to her, Emerson. She is trying to play her final hand while she doesn't have a single ace left up her sleeve."

Elsie's eyes shifted to Jensen. "My hand is spent, guardian. Even the help from the damned didn't bring me any closer to my victory. What benefit befalls me to lie now, when the dead lie silent?"

"Enough. Perhaps he was right. Maybe you do need to be placed under some kind of watch."

"Watch me all you will. Meanwhile, the loose ends of this saga will go on to fray your efforts here tonight. Some might call that negligence. Seems like quite a sin. Things left unresolved will leave you incapable of letting go. Ask your mother. It is why she's still in limbo. There's this odd little saying I once heard from a seer: 'If you sin in moderation, then hell comes for you much later.'"

Familiar words from a familiar mouth. Jensen felt her powers surge as her emotions got the better of her. Still, just as she was about to do something she would have regretted,

Emerson placed his hand on her shoulder. "Listen, I know this may not be easy to hear, but I think she has a point."

"*What?* You looked about ready to shackle her two seconds ago."

"Until I started thinking about it. Jensen, we may have averted chaos, but some things were never resolved. Five witches were raised as undead powerhouses at the start of all this, and now that I think about it, none of them were ever brought to heel. And then there is Friar Ambrose. He placed his life on the line to acquire the information that he did. The way his handwriting changed was ominous. I think something happened to him."

A chill ran down her spine as the truth of his observation sank in. He was right. Loose ends still spoiled the pattern by which they had solved the mystery and overcome the crisis. As her mind raced to work through the possibilities, another oversight dawned on her. Instinctively, her hand shot up to her ear to feel the pearl earring given to her for protection. She was still wearing it. She reprimanded herself for not asking a critical question sooner. There was one Gate Guardian who was not among the coven tonight. "There's something else," she began. "What in the hell happened to my aunt?"

ABOUT THE AUTHOR

Renee Joiner has been in love with the supernatural for longer than she can remember, so it is no surprise that she is an author of paranormal urban fantasy. Although she discovered her passion for writing when she was only twelve years old, she didn't make her writing debut until many years into the future. Adventurous and fun-loving, she enjoys traveling to new places, exploring new sights and meeting new people. Thus, she delights in creating fantastical worlds that are sure to give her readers an escape from the real world while simultaneously providing thrilling entertainment.

Besides her special knack for writing, you'll also find a passion for metaphysics spirituality which she has been nurturing for over four decades. Renee hails from New York and currently resides with her husband in their empty nest —unless you count their three adorable fur babies—in Florida. She enjoys adding to her sea of knowledge and thus spends her free time learning new things.

To find out more about Renee Joiner, feel free to visit her **official website.**

facebook.com/reneejoinerauthor

twitter.com/iamreneejoiner

instagram.com/reneejoinerauthor

amazon.com/author/reneejoiner

SERIES BY RENEE

Dark Huntress Series
Glen Cove
The Witch
The Djinn
The Countess

Thorne Sisters Chronicles
Possessed by Magic
Reincarnated by Magic
Immortal by Magic

Magic of the Night
Raven Magic

SIGN UP TO RECEIVE MY
NEWLETTER FOR ALL THE
LATEST UPDATES AND SPECIALS!

RENEEJOINERAUTHOR.COM/NEWSLETTER

Thank You...

Thank you for reading my book!
I really appreciate all of your feedback and I love to hear what you have to say. Please leave your review at your favorite retailer!